Meet the Pebbles

See that car driving over the bridge?
Inside it are some Pebbles.

I don't mean pebbles like stones. What I mean is a family called The Pebbles.

This is what they look like:

Melvin

Violet

Deirdre

Norman

Sorry if you're listening to an audiobook, by the way.

A SUPER WEIRD! MYSTERY™

"Danger" at D⊙nut Diner

Jim Smith

Som ..

'Will make you laugh out loud, cringe and snigger, all at the same time'
—LoveReading4Kids

SCHOLASTIC
Lollies
LAUGH OUT LOUD
BOOK AWARDS
PRIZE-WINNING AUTHOR

'Very funny and cheeky'
—Booktictac, Guardian Online Review

Waterstones Children's Book Prize Shortlistee!

'WHAT'S NOT TO LOVE?'
—Sun

'I LAUGHED SO MUCH, I THOUGHT THAT I WAS GOING TO BURST!'
Finbar, aged 9

'The review of the eight year old boy in our house...
"Can I keep it to give to a friend?"
Best recommendation you can get' —Observer

'HUGELY ENJOYABLE, SURREAL CH...
—G...

The Roald Dahl
FUNNY PRIZE

C334470452

...03

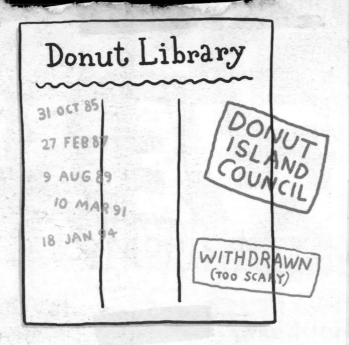

Donut Library

31 OCT 85
27 FEB 87
9 AUG 89
10 MAR 91
18 JAN 94

DONUT ISLAND COUNCIL

WITHDRAWN
(TOO SCARY)

Massive thanks to my editor, Liz Bankes, for all her genius help with this book, and to my amazing publisher Ali Dougal and brilliant agent Caroline Sheldon for always being so keel. And to Jenny and Woody for telling me when something's rubbish, and coming up with the title!

First published in Great Britain 2020 by Egmont UK Ltd, 2 Minster Court, London EC3R 7BB

Text and illustration copyright © Jim Smith 2020
The moral rights of Jim Smith have been asserted.

ISBN 978 1 4502 9545 1

barryloser.com
www.egmont.co.uk

A CIP catalogue record for this title is available from the British Library

Printed and bound in Great Britain by the CPI Group

67191/001

EGMONT
We bring stories to life

MIX
Paper from responsible sources
FSC® C020471

The Pebbles were driving from Hokum City towards a completely round island.

On one side of the island, three huge clumps of earth had fallen into the sea, making it look like a giant fish had taken a bite out of it or something.

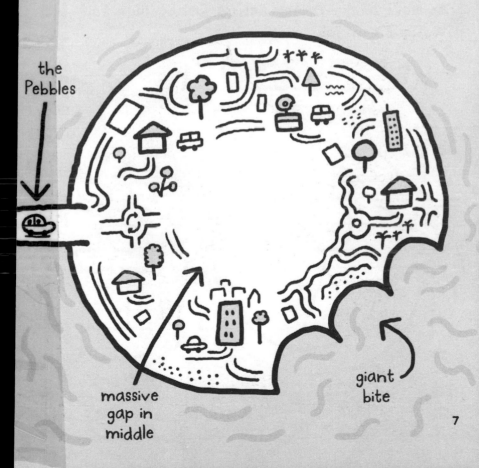

the Pebbles

massive gap in middle

giant bite

'Donut Island here we come!' grinned Deirdre Pebble, peering into the rear-view mirror. 'Looking forward to your new life, kids?'

Swirling black thunderclouds rumbled in the sky above and lightning flickered like a half-broken bulb.

'Nope,' said Violet Pebble, who was the oldest and most annoying of the two. 'I don't see why I have to leave all my friends behind just because you got a stupid new job.'

'Violet!' cried Norman Pebble in his trying-to-be-a-dad voice. 'Your mother's new job is NOT stupid.'

Melvin Pebble, who was sitting next to his big sister, wiggled his bum in its seat. 'I can't wait,' he said.

Violet rolled her eyes. 'It's alright for you,' she said. 'Your friends are all complete losers.'

A bolt of lightning shot out of a cloud, striking the middle of the island with an enormous . . .

BOOM!

'WAAAHHH!!!' screamed the Pebbles, as the car swerved left and right.

'So, my announcement,' said Melvin, once they'd all settled down again. 'I have decided that from now on I'm gonna be the coolest kid in town.'

Violet laughed. 'Oh per-lease,' she said.
'You couldn't be cool if you were stuck inside a fridge. With sunglasses on. And gel in your hair. Wearing a t-shirt that said I AM COOL on it.'

'Oh yeah?' said Melvin. 'Well I wouldn't even be able to fit inside a fridge. Unless you took out all the shelves. But even then it'd be a squeeze. So who's laughing now?'

'Not me,' said Violet, yawning as the car trundled off the bridge, past an enormous billboard.

This is what it said:

WELCOME TO DONUT ISLAND

Violet stared through her rain-splattered window at the billboard. 'The boringest town in the universe,' she grumbled.

Of course, she'd never've said that if she'd known what was going to happen in the rest of this book.

Rhubarb Plonsky

The Pebble family car drove up to its new house.
Not that a car can have a house exactly, but you
know what I mean.

Melvin jumped out and stretched his legs.
The thunderstorm had finished and he could just
about see the moon hanging in the sky, like a
gigantic chopped-in-half donut.

half donut   half moon

'Feels great to stretch your legs, doesn't it?' grinned Norman Pebble, bending over to touch his smelly feet, and his bum peeped out of its trousers.

'Not really,' said Melvin, as his mum staggered up to the house carrying a giant cardboard box. Clinking around inside was her collection of empty jam jars.

'You can never have too many jam jars,' smiled Deirdre. Not that anyone had mentioned them or anything. She just liked talking about her jam jars.

Norman looked at his wife. 'You do realise jam jars are supposed to have something inside them, don't you, Deirdre?' he said.

'It's tragic really,' said Melvin, watching his mum. He walked round to the boot of the car and heaved out a box himself.

This one had **'Melv's stuff'** written on the side.

The flaps were half-open and the tops of a million little toy packets fluttered in the breeze.

'SHHH!' shushed a noise from behind him and Melvin twizzled round.

In front of him sat a fat little bush. Its leaves were rattling like it was shaking with fear. Thunder rumbled in the distance, and Melvin giggled, nervously.

'What's wrong, little fella?' he asked the bush, sort of as a joke. 'You scared of the storm?'

'Please be quiet!' said the bush, and Melvin stumbled backwards.

'Th-that bush!' he stuttered. 'It's alive!'

All of a sudden a girl's head poked out, about the same age as Melvin's.

'**Waaah!** It's got a head as well!' screamed Melvin.

'SHUSH!' shushed the girl. 'Would you keep it down? I'm waiting for my new next-door neighbours to arrive.'

Melvin breathed a sigh of relief. 'Oh,' he smiled. 'I think that might be . . .'

'QUIET!'

whispered the girl. 'I've been hiding in this bush all blooming weekend and the last thing I need is you lot scaring them away.'

Deirdre plonked her jam jars down by the front door and walked over to the girl. 'We're the Pebbles!' she smiled.

The girl went silent for a millisecond, then clicked her fingers.

'Hey, you're my new next-door neighbours!' she grinned. 'My name's Rhubarb Plonsky. Very nice to meet you!'

The next chapter

Deirdre Pebble chuckled at how ridiculous her new next-door neighbour's name was, even though her own name was Deirdre Pebble.

'Very nice to meet you too, Rhubarb Plonsky,' she said, putting her hands on her hips. 'I'm Deirdre and that's my husband Norman.'

'And those two are Violet and Melvin,' she said, pointing at them. Violet was still slouched in the back of the car. 'Say hello, kids.'

'Hello kids,' said Violet, and Melvin sniggled.

'Hello, Rhubarb Plonsky,' he said.

Rhubarb sniffed the air. 'Is that a Hokum City accent?' she asked.

Violet raised an eyebrow. 'That's a pretty good shnoz you've got there,' she said.

Rhubarb marched straight up to Melvin and did another sniff.

'Stinks, doesn't he,' said Violet.

Rhubarb shook her head. 'It's not that,' she said. 'It's something else. Do you like mysteries, Melvin?'

'Erm, I dunno,' said Melvin.

'Hmmm, we'll see,' said Rhubarb, pincering one of the little plastic toy packets from Melvin's cardboard box. 'What are these things, anyway?'

Melvin pulled the box away and pushed the cardboard flaps shut.

'NOTHING!'

he said.

Violet slid out of the car and wandered over. 'That's my little brother's collection of toy bags.'

'You collect toy bags?' asked Rhubarb.

Melvin nodded. 'And the toys inside them,' he said.

Rhubarb stroked her chin. 'But none of the bags were open,' she said.

'Melvin doesn't open the bags,' said Violet.
'He's way too cool for that.'

'I like guessing what's inside them,' said Melvin,
pulling one out of the box and giving it a fiddle.
'Anyway, the packets are more interesting than
the toys half the time.'

Rhubarb thought for a second. 'Plus I suppose
all the excitement's gone once you've opened it,'
she said.

"Exactly!"

smiled Melvin.

Violet stared down at the two of them.
'She's almost as cool as you, Melv,' she chuckled.
'Say, be a good little brother and grab my bags
from the car, wouldya?'

Rhubarb opened her mouth. 'What's it like?'
she said. 'Hokum City, I mean.'

Violet looked around. 'Better than this place,'
she grumbled.

Rhubarb's face went all serious
and she leaned forwards.
'Donut's not an ordinary
town,' she whispered, so
only Melvin could hear.

'What does that mean?'
asked Melvin. 'Not that
I care or anything,' he added,
trying to sound a bit cooler.

'I'll tell you tomorrow,' said Rhubarb,
marching off, but not very far, seeing
as she only lived next door.

Donut High Street

It was the next morning and Melvin was walking to school with Rhubarb Plonsky.

As they turned onto Donut High Street, Melvin peered around at the dusty old shops. Each one had the word 'Donut' written on its sign, then the name of the thing it sold next to that.

There was Donut Butchers, Donut Books and a shop called Donut Toys. Next door to that was Donut Funerals and across the street, next to Donut Magazines, was Donut Hamburgers.

'Donut Hairdressers,' said Melvin, reading what the nearest shop was called. 'Who goes in there, little hairy donuts who want a haircut?'

Rhubarb sniggered. 'Ooh, I like people who try and be funny!' she said, giving him a nudge, and he boinked into a blue lamppost which had 'Donut Electric Co' written on it in dented-in letters.

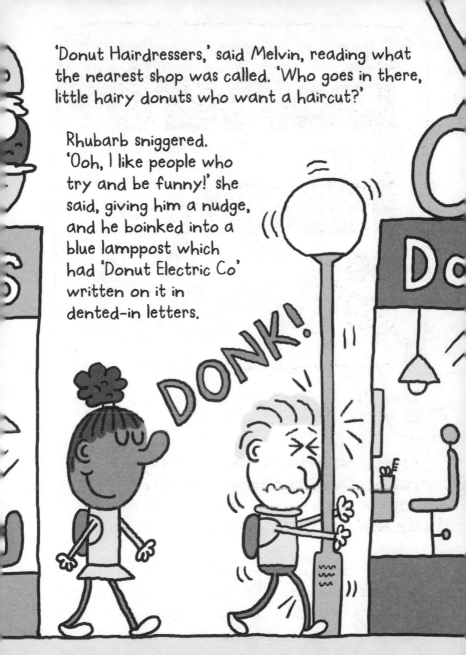

DONK!

At the end of the road stood a low, round building with an enormous plastic donut sitting on top of it.

The words 'DONUT DINER' were printed on the gigantic snack in huge yellow capitals.

Behind the building was a great big circle of scrubby-looking land with a wire fence all the way round it.

'That's where the hole used to be,' said Rhubarb, spotting where Melvin was looking.

'The hole?' said Melvin.

Rhubarb nodded. 'Why do you think it's called Donut Island?' she said. 'A donut's not a donut without a hole!'

'Unless it's a jam one,' said Melvin. 'So what happened to this hole?'

'They filled it in,' said Rhubarb. 'Spose it was a bit dangerous, having a great big hole sitting there in the middle of town.'

Melvin zoomed his eyes in on the filled-in hole. There was a zig-zaggy crack in the middle, kind of like a lightning bolt had hit it.

He remembered the enormous

BOOM!

from the night before and a bubble popped in his tummy, like he was a can of donut-flavour cola or something.

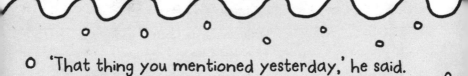

'That thing you mentioned yesterday,' he said. 'About Donut not being an ordinary town . . .'

Rhubarb smiled. 'Bet you were thinking about that all night, weren't you?'

'Not in the slightest at all,' said Melvin, trying to sound cool. 'What did it mean, though?'

Rhubarb leaned towards him. 'Do you like mysteries?' she asked.

Another blooming chapter

'Do I like mysteries?' said Melvin. 'Didn't you ask me that already?'

'I dunno, did I?' said Rhubarb, stuffing her hand into her rucksack and pulling out a few sheets of folded-in-half paper that'd been stapled together into a homemade newspaper.

'Ta da!' said Rhubarb. 'All the latest Donut Island mysteries, hot off the press every Friday morning!'

'What is it?' asked Melvin, even though it was pretty obvious.

'It's my newspaper, stupid!' said Rhubarb.

Melvin peered at the hand-drawn headline on the front page. This is what it said:

The Mystery Of The Cat That Disappeared In Mysterious Circumstances

Rhubarb scratched her bum. 'Ooh that's a good one,' she said. 'There was this cat right, and it went missing . . .'

The Daily Donut

Edited by Rhubarb Plonsky

THE MYSTERY OF THE CAT THAT DISAPPEARED IN MYSTERIOUS CIRCUMSTANCES

Old granny Doreen Shminkle's cat Olive went missing last night, it has been revealed. 'One minute she was on my lap, the next she'd disappeared,' said Doreen, waggling her hands when she said the word 'disappeared'. CONTINUES INSIDE!

33

'What happened?' said Melvin.

Rhubarb leaned forwards, dialling the volume on her voice down to a three. 'Turns out,' she whispered, 'the cat'd gone for a really long walk.'

'That's it?' said Melvin.

'There's even better ones than that,' said Rhubarb, flicking to another page.

The headline on this one said:

THE STRANGE CASE OF THE GRANNY THAT GOT STUCK INSIDE A PHOTO

'Okay I admit it, that's pretty weird,' said Melvin. 'So what happened?'

'The granny hadn't got stuck at all,' smiled Rhubarb. 'All she'd done was pop to the loo. Meanwhile, her husband decided she'd been sucked into the picture frame on the mantelpiece.'

'Well that makes sense,' said Melvin.

Rhubarb turned to a different page. This one read:

The Curious Incident Of The Murdered Hamster

'Let me guess,' Melvin said. 'It died of old age?'

'Ooh, you're good,' said Rhubarb.

'I think I'm going off mysteries,' said Melvin.

'But mysteries are the best!' said Rhubarb.
'Tell you what, we're having a Daily Donut
meeting at mine after school. Why don't you
come along?'

'Let me check my diary,' said Melvin, as they
walked up to the gates of Donut Juniors.

DONUT JUNIORS

'Follow me,' said Rhubarb, leading Melvin into the school and down a long hallway lined with yellow metal lockers. She pushed a door open into a classroom and walked straight up to the front row.

Rhubarb plonked her bum down in a chair next to a bendy-looking boy with straight black hair and glasses.

'Melvin, this is Yoshi Fujikawa,' she said. 'Yoshi works with me on The Daily Donut. He wrote that dead hamster story I showed you.'

Yoshi, who was scribbling something in a notepad, stopped writing and smiled at Melvin. 'Took a lot out of me, that one,' he said, pushing his glasses up his nose. 'I'm working on a similarly disturbing piece as we speak.'

'Oh yeah?' said Melvin, not holding out much hope for it, after what he'd read earlier.

'Yeah, somebody dropped a slice of cucumber on the floor in the canteen last Friday,' he said. 'But nobody knows who . . .'

'Okay,' said Melvin. 'Hey Rhubarb, are there any cool kids in this school?'

Just then, the door opened and a really old-looking boy with a moustache walked in. 'Evening, gang,' he boomed in a deep voice, and Melvin realised he wasn't a boy, he was their teacher.

'Look who's here, Sir,' said Rhubarb, pointing at Melvin.

'Is it Monday morning already?' gasped the teacher, glancing at his watch. 'Last time I looked it was Friday afternoon. Oh well, in that case you must be the new kid. Very nice to meet you, Melvin Pebble. I'm Mr Thursday!'

Melvin pretended to laugh at Mr Thursday's joke. 'Nice to meet you, Sir,' he said, looking round the room.

((AND THAT'S)) ((WHEN HE)) ((SPOTTED)) ((THEM.))

Sitting on the other side of the aisle, in the back row, were three cool-looking kids. 'Hey, who are they?' whispered Melvin to Rhubarb, and she rolled her eyes.

'Hector Frisbee, Dirk Measles and Marjorie Pinecone,' she said.

'They call themselves The Cool Doods,' said Yoshi, scribbling the words down in his notepad and holding it up so Melvin could see the stupid way they spelled 'Dudes'.

The Cool Doods

Mr Thursday sat down at his desk as Melvin stared at Hector Frisbee.

His trainers were white with silver zig-zags on the sides.

His jeans were the really expensive ones Melvin had been begging his mum to buy him all year and his jumper was black with a little yellow bottle-top logo on the chest, which everyone knew was the coolest logo ever.

'I hope everyone's been looking after you, Melvin?' said Mr Thursday.

'Too late for us, Teach,' sneered Dirk Measles. 'Looks like the geeks have got their claws into him already.'

'Thank you, Measles,' said Mr Thursday, and Marjorie Pinecone smirked.

'I spose Rhubarb's told you all about her mysterious yawnpaper,' she said to Melvin. 'What's it called again? Oh yeah, The Daily Do-NOT.'

Rhubarb tutted. 'It's The Daily Do-NUT,' she snapped. 'Maybe if you'd actually bothered to read it, you'd know that.'

Marjorie smiled. 'Cool Rool number one: Reading is for losers,' she said.

Dirk pretended he was about to cry. 'Rhubarb's bullying us again, Mr Thurs,' he warbled, and Hector Frisbee shook his head.

'Please ignore my sidekicks, Melvin,' he said. 'I'm Hector, by the way. If you need anything while you're settling in, just let me know.'

'Thanks,' said Melvin, trying to think if there was anything he needed right now, apart from the wee he'd been holding in since halfway down Donut High Street.

Marjorie nudged Hector. 'We probably shouldn't be talking to him, you know,' she said. 'Cool Rool number two: No talking to Daily Donut losers.'

THE COOL DOODS'
COOL ROOLS

1. Reading is for losers
2. No talking to Daily Donut losers
3. Never get excited
4. Check hair a lot
5. Walk like you can't be bothered
6. Memorise The Cool Rools
7. No playing games
8. Yawn when person talking to you
9. Turn page over for more...

Rhubarb rolled her eyes and tapped Melvin on the shoulder. 'Everyone thinks The Cool Doods are so cool,' she whispered.

'But they're not,' said Yoshi. 'They're actually really boring.'

Melvin nodded. 'Er, okay. Thanks, guys,' he said, flipping open his exercise book.

Then he pulled his favourite silver pen out of his pencil case and started doodling 'The Cool Doods' in his best bubble writing.

Shortest chapter EVER

All of a sudden it was the end of school. Actually, it wasn't all of a sudden at all, it took hours.

'Coming to our Daily Donut meeting then, Melv?' asked Rhubarb, grabbing her rucksack out of her locker, which was covered in cuttings from her newspaper.

Hector walked past with Dirk and Marjorie. 'Come on, let's get out of here, Doods,' he said. 'Thought we could go down Donut Diner and play it cool.'

Melvin turned to Hector. 'Hey, I could come along if you wanted,' he said. 'I haven't been to the diner yet.'

Hector smiled. 'Not this time, Pebbles,' he said.

The Cool Doods strolled off and Melvin waved. 'Okay, see you later, guys!' he called, as Rhubarb grabbed his sleeve.

'Come on Melvin,' she said, heading off to her house. 'The meeting starts in ten minutes!'

Mrs Plonsky

'Melvin, meet my mum,' said Rhubarb, walking into her kitchen with him and Yoshi ten minutes later.

'Pleasure to meet you, Mrs Plonsky,' smiled Melvin, acting all nice and polite.

'Ooh, my new mini next-door neighbour!' said Mrs Plonsky, looking up from her crossword. 'I met your parents earlier, what a lovely couple!'

'Are you sure you met the right ones?' said Melvin, and Mrs Plonsky chuckled.

'Do you like mysteries, Melvin?' she asked, just like Rhubarb had that morning.

Rhubarb gave her mum a cuddle. 'Mum was the editor of The Daily Donut when she was a kid, too,' she said.

'Ooh, that reminds me,' said Mrs Plonsky to Rhubarb. 'I talked to the people at Donut Town Hall today and they said next Tuesday is still on.'

Rhubarb turned to Melvin. 'I've got this talk thing next week,' she explained. 'It's nothing special.'

'Don't be so modest, Rubes!' said Yoshi. 'She's doing a whole great big presentation about being an editor of a newspaper and everything.'

Rhubarb's mum nodded. 'I've put flyers up all over Donut,' she said. 'The place'll be full up. You should come along, Melvin. It's gonna be fantastic!'

'Of course I'll come,' said Melvin.

EXCITIN
TALK!

Mrs Plonsky smiled at Yoshi. 'How are you, Yosh?' she asked. 'Still scribbling away?'

'You bet, Thelma,' said Yoshi, patting his notepad. 'There's been a major development in the Mystery Of The Dropped Cucumber Slice, in fact.'

'Right,' said Rhubarb, opening a door and clicking a light switch. 'It's meeting time!'

Daily Donut HQ

Melvin followed Rhubarb and Yoshi down some creaky steps into a dusty old basement. 'Welcome to Daily Donut HQ,' smiled Rhubarb, and Melvin looked around.

It was dark apart from a single lightbulb, which flickered like the lightning in the storm the night before.

Over on the other side
of the room were some
green metal shelves,
stacked with what looked
like old newspapers.

Melvin went and picked a
copy up. 'The Daily Donut,'
it said at the top in big
red letters.

This paper didn't look homemade like the one
Rhubarb had shown him that morning though.
It was printed like a real newspaper and had
ten times as many pages.

'They're my mum's old copies,' said Rhubarb.

'Are you telling me The Daily Donut used to be an actual thing?' said Melvin. 'Not that yours isn't, of course.'

Rhubarb smiled. 'It's okay, I know what you mean,' she said. 'Yeah, back when Mum was editor, it was a real-life school newspaper. They had an office at school with printers and everything.'

'Were the mysteries still as rubbish?' asked Melvin, trying to be funny.

Yoshi's nose drooped. 'Hey, our mysteries aren't rubbish,' he said.

'School won't pay for us to print them any more,' Rhubarb said. 'I spose my stories just aren't as good as hers . . .'

'Oh, right,' said Melvin, feeling a bit bad about his joke. He looked down at the copy he was holding and started to read it.

The Daily Donut

THE STRANGE CASE OF THE MYSTERIOUS SUPER MOON

'A delivery van drove straight into Donut Island's famous hole last night,' he said in his best newspapery voice. 'The driver, who jumped to safety at the last second, blamed the accident on a strange giant moon.'

Yoshi pointed to the next part of the story.

' "All of a sudden, I spotted a crater on the moon open up," said Trevor Doofus, the driver of the van, who is a short man with a very hairy face. "A beam of green light shot out of it, aiming straight into the hole on Donut Island".'

'Blimey,' said Melvin, as Yoshi carried on reading.

' "I could feel the van being dragged towards the hole," said Mr Doofus, beads of sweat zig-zagging down his furry forehead. "So I opened the door and dived out. Everything after that is just a blur".'

Melvin shook his head. 'That can't be true,' he said.

'I wonder what was in that hairy little man's van,' said Yoshi. 'Spooky to imagine it lying at the bottom of the hole, isn't it?'

'No,' said Melvin, even though it completely was. He crossed the idea out in his brain and flicked to another page.

This is what it said at the top:

THE MYSTERY OF THE HEADLESS WEREHOG

The story was about a strange spiky creature with no head that was lolloping around Donut Island, eating people's milk bottles.

'Sightings of the beast are rare,' Melvin read out loud. 'But numbers seem to increase around the time of a full moon.'

Yoshi's eyes opened wide. 'It sounds like a werewolf,' he said. 'Except more hedgehoggy.'

'And with no head!' grinned Rhubarb, grabbing a torch off her desk and shining it under her face. It was one of those torches with no batteries where you have to pump the handle to make it light up. 'Do you like my torch, Melv?' she asked. 'It's eco!'

push down →

this lights up

Eco Bright

There was a scratching noise in the corner of the room.

'What was that?' said Melvin.

Rhubarb chuckled. 'Oh, that's the mice,' she said, pointing her torch at them and pumping its handle. Melvin spotted a tail waggling off into the darkness. 'Me and mum can't bring ourselves to get rid of them.'

'Maybe they're not mice,'
said Yoshi. 'Maybe they're
WEREHOGS!'

'Ha, ha, very unfunny,' said Melvin,
sliding the newspaper back onto
the shelf. 'Hey, why don't we
go down to Donut Diner?' he said,
wondering what the Cool Doods
were up to, but also trying to
change the subject from
milk-bottle-eating
werehogs.

Yoshi pulled his notepad out of his pocket.
'Focus, Pebbles,' he said.

Rhubarb scratched her earlobe. 'What was that
cucmber development you were talking about
earlier, Fujikawa?' she asked, and Yoshi flipped
his little book open.

65

'Ah yes,' he said, finding the right page. 'I was having a good snoop around the canteen after lunch today and you'll never guess what I found.'

'The cucumber slice?' said Rhubarb.

'That's right!' grinned Yoshi. 'It was still in exactly the same spot as last Friday. I started to pace up and down the canteen, trying to work out who'd dropped the thing. And that's when I noticed it'd disappeared - right in front of my eyes!'

'You know what this means, don't you?' he said.

Melvin shook his head as Yoshi opened his mouth.

'It means it was a . . .

Ghost cucumber!'

Rhubarb sniffed the air. 'I smell a mystery!' she smiled. 'Now, where do we think this ghost cucumber came from in the first place?'

Melvin perched his bum on one of the newspaper shelves and it creaked. 'It didn't come from anywhere,' he said. 'Because there's no such thing as ghost cucumbers.'

Yoshi looked at Rhubarb, who was staring at Melvin.

'Yoshi, what's the first rule of Daily Donut Club?' she asked, not taking her eyes off her new next-door neighbour.

Yoshi pointed at a piece of
paper taped up on the wall.

Daily Donut Club
Rules

1. Don't Poo-Poo Anything
2. Be Nosey
3. Trust Your Hunch
4. Don't Trust Your Hunch
5. Listen To Your Friends
6. Everything's A Mystery
7. Nothing Is A Waste Of
Time

Yoshi twizzled round to face Melvin. 'You'll never solve a mystery if you poo-poo it, Pebbles,' he said.

Melvin held his hands up. 'Okay, okay, no poo-poo-ing,' he said, and he tried to think where you might be able to get a ghost cucumber from. 'A cucumber shop?'

DONUT CUCUMBERS

Rhubarb giggled. 'You don't get CUCUMBER shops, Melvin,' she said. 'Ooh, what about a ghost shop?'

'I don't remember seeing a ghost shop on Donut High Street,' laughed Melvin nervously.

'Well you wouldn't be able to see it, would you,' said Rhubarb. 'It'd be invisible.'

Yoshi twitched his nose. 'Wait a minute, wouldn't ghost cucumbers come from a ghost farm?'

'Focus, Yoshi,' said Melvin, mainly to stop all the talk about ghosts.

Rhubarb looked at him 'You okay, Melv?' she asked. 'It's alright to be scared, you know.'

'I'm not scared!' laughed Melvin, as the door to the basement creaked open and the shadow of a giant claw appeared, projected onto the brick wall.

The sound of hooves clip-clopping down the stairs echoed round the room.

'WAAAHHH!!! GHOST COW!!!'

screamed Melvin, leaping into Rhubarb's arms.

The hooves got closer. Or maybe they were Mrs Plonsky's shoes.

'Only me, kiddywinkles!' she smiled, peering out of the darkness. 'Anyone want a snack?'

Yoshi chuckled. 'Got any ghost biscuits?' he asked, as Melvin slipped out of Rhubarb's arms.

'No thanks, Mum,' she said, and Mrs Plonsky clip-clopped back up the steps.

71

'I knew that wasn't a ghost cow, by the way,'
said Melvin.

Rhubarb smiled. 'Sure you did,' she said, looking
at what she'd written on her scrap of paper,
which was completely nothing.

'Okay, so there's no cucumber shop in Donut.
And the ghost shop would be too hard to
find. So that leaves . . .'

'Donut Supermarket!' said Yoshi.

Donut Super- market

It was getting dark by the time Melvin, Rhubarb and Yoshi skidded to a stop outside Donut Supermarket, and the moon was hanging in the sky. It was bigger than the night before, but only by a sliver.

Rhubarb stopped pumping her torch handle as they walked through the big sliding doors into the supermarket, which was as bright as the inside of a fridge.

'Phew, that torch doesn't half take it out of you,' she panted.

'Excuse me, Madam,' said Yoshi, strolling up to a woman in a brown Donut Supermarket uniform. She had a name tag with 'Glenda' written on it. 'Can you point me towards the ghost cucumber aisle?'

Glenda peered down at Yoshi. 'Halloween is next month,' she growled.

Rhubarb peered around, spotting a sign in the distance saying 'VEGETABLES'. 'This way!' she said, speeding towards it.

She sprinted past the sausages, hung a left at a pyramid of fungal nail treatments and turned right onto a corridor of green stuff. 'Cucumbers are down the end,' she called, skating along the shiny floor.

'Ooh, two for one on courgettes,' said Yoshi, as they started to search.

Melvin pointed at an empty shelf and pretended to grab something off it. 'Check it out - a ghost cucumber!' he said, holding up a handful of air.

'No poo-poo-ing, Melv,' chuckled Rhubarb, peering down at the bottom shelf. And then she stopped. 'Ah,' she said.

'What is it, Plonsky?' asked Yoshi. 'Have you found a ghost cucumber?'

Rhubarb was staring at Yoshi's feet. 'What's that slimy trail leading up to your shoe, Yosh?' she asked.

Yoshi lifted his foot and looked down. 'Ah,' he said, peeling a completely squashed slice of cucumber off the bottom of his shoe. 'Looks like I maybe trod on it in the canteen.'

Melvin twizzled round on the spot and started marching towards the door. 'I can't believe it,' he said. 'Talk about poo-poo-ing. You just poo-pooed my whole afternoon!'

He walked back through the sliding doors and stopped outside the supermarket, waiting for Rhubarb and Yoshi to catch up.

Donut Supermarket

'Another mystery solved!' smiled Rhubarb, appearing next to him. 'Yoshi, you wanna write that one up?'

'Already on it, Boss,' said Yoshi.

Melvin blinked. 'You're both crazy!' he cried. 'For starters, that wasn't a mystery. And for main course, you didn't solve it!'

Yoshi was scribbling in his notepad again. 'The Mysterious Case Of The Slice Of Ghost Cucumber,' he said, reading out what he was writing. 'It was a dark and stormy night . . .'

Melvin held his palm out. 'It isn't even pitter-pattering,' he said.

'There's nothing wrong with a bit of exaggeration, Melv,' said Rhubarb. 'All the great editors know that.'

'Yeah well,' said Melvin, and he was just about to march off again when he spotted something that made him gasp.

Boring old bus stop

'Look!' cried Melvin, pointing towards a bus stop.

Yoshi peered up from his notepad. 'What about it, Melvin?' he said. 'It's just a boring old bus stop.'

'I'm not talking about the bus stop,' said Melvin. 'I'm talking about the advert next to it!'

'Looks like their eyes glow in the dark,' said Yoshi, pointing at a bit of writing that said 'Their Eyes Glow In The Dark!'

'I wonder if they come in bags,' said Rhubarb, giving Melvin a nudge.

'Ooh, I hope so,' he said, zooming in on the tiny writing at the bottom of the poser.

'Offer starts this Friday,' it said.

'But today's only Monday,' said Melvin. 'I dunno if I can wait that long.'

Rhubarb patted him on the back. 'Don't worry, Melvin,' she smiled. 'Me and Yoshi will keep you busy.'

Doesn't time fly

You know when you have to wait a whole week for Donut Hole Monsters to come out, and the only way to get through it is by traipsing around behind Rhubarb and Yoshi, investigating their little mysteries, even though you'd prefer to be playing it cool with The Cool Doods?

That's what Melvin did for the next three days.

Like on Tuesday, when he really wanted to follow The Cool Doods down to the adventure playground in Donut Park after school, but they said there was only room for three people in the whole place, so he hung out with Rhubarb and Yoshi instead, trying to solve The Mystery Of The Grandad Who Turned Into A Tree.*

TUESDAY...

*The grandad was walking down the road when he passed behind a horse chestnut, bent down to do up his shoelace and got stuck in that position for three hours.

Or on Wednesday, when Melvin invited The Cool Doods for tea round his house, but they were all washing their hair at that exact same time, so Rhubarb and Yoshi came instead.

'Hey look,' said Yoshi, pointing out of the window at the leaves falling off a tree, and he whipped his notebook out and wrote 'The Strange Occurrence Of All The Leaves Suddenly Falling Off Of Every Tree In The Whole of Donut.'*

*It was Autumn.

Then on Thursday, when Mr Thursday let all the kids go home five minutes early because it was his favourite day, and The Cool Doods went to Donut Arcade on the high street but Melvin couldn't go because they said there was already a person called Melvin who worked at the Arcade and there was a rule on Donut Island that only one Melvin could be in any single building at a time.

THURSDAY...

MELVIN

MELVIN

SLIME INVADERS!

'Why don't you help me and Yoshi instead?' said Rhubarb, so Melvin went round her house and finished off that week's edition of The Daily Donut then photocopied it ten times to give out to all the kids who didn't want it the next day at school.

Still still Thursday

It was Thursday evening and Donut News was on the telly. A bearded man was talking about the filled-in hole in the middle of the island and how it seemed to be cracking open for some reason.

'How you doing, Vi?' said Melvin, slumping onto the sofa next to his big sister.

'Yeah great,' said Violet, itching her nose.
'Really great.' She glanced at her brother. 'You?'

Melvin sighed. 'Not bad,' he said. 'I've been up
to my ears in Daily Donut stuff.'

Violet changed the channel. 'The Daily Donut,
eh,' she chuckled.

'Tell me about it,' said Melvin. 'Don't get me wrong.
It's fun hanging out with Rhubarb and Yoshi.
They're just a bit geeky.'

'Huh,' said Violet. 'So what happened to you being
the coolest kid in town?'

Melvin shook his head. 'I'm trying,' he said.
'But The Cool Doods won't let me join their gang.'

'The Cool Doods,' said Violet. 'They sound
REALLY cool.'

'Yeah, they are,' said Melvin, even
though he knew his sister was
being sarcastic.

He looked out of the window at the moon,
which was almost three-quarters full now.

'I just need a bit more time,' he mumbled to
himself. 'You wait - I'll be a Cool Dood soon.'

Never get excited

Somebody changed the channel again and it was Friday afternoon.

'See Melv, I told you it'd go fast,' said Rhubarb, strolling up to Donut Diner with him and Yoshi. She still had three copies of The Daily Donut tucked under her arm.

'Free Daily Donut?' she smiled, waggling a copy in the face of a passing granny.

'No thanks, love,' warbled the old lady, doddering away at minus-twelve millimetres per hour.

Melvin stared up at the great big plastic donut sitting on top of the building in front of him. 'Donut Hole Monsters here we come!' he giggled, doing a little bum wiggle.

Marjorie Pinecone wandered over with Dirk and Hector. 'Don't you know Cool Rool number three, Pebbles?' she smirked.

'Ooh I do, I do,' said Dirk, almost weeing himself with excitement. 'It's **Never Get Excited!**'

Melvin ran his hand through his hair like it was a comb made out of fingers. 'Chill out, Dirk' he said, smiling at Hector. 'It's only a stupid donut shop.'

Yoshi patted Melvin's shoulder and chuckled. 'Nice save, Melvin,' he said.

DONUT HOLE MONSTERS HAVE ARRIVED!

boomed the banner outside the entrance to Donut Diner, and Melvin felt a Donut Cola bubble pop inside his tummy.

'Hey, I've got an idea,' he said. 'Why don't we all sit together? Seeing as it's a special day and everything.'

Hector chuckled. 'You crack me up, Melvin,' he said, pushing the doors of Donut Diner open, and Melvin

GASPED!

But only so you'd read the next chapter.

Donut Diner

Donut Diner was about the size of a regular donut shop, except shaped like a giant donut. It had orange booths all the way round the edge and a big glass counter in the middle.

'Welcome to Donut Diner!' said the man standing behind it. Pinned to his orange polyester t-shirt was a badge with 'Dwayne' written on it.

Melvin stared through the glass counter at the racks of donuts and waggled his hand around in his pocket, feeling for a coin.

'Good old Deirdre Pebble!' he smiled, pulling out the pound his mum had given him that morning.

'Put your money away,' said Rhubarb, marching up to the counter. 'These donuts are on me.'

She smiled at Dwayne. 'Three chocolate ones, please.'

'Ooh, thanks Rhubarb,' said Melvin. 'Erm, I suppose,' he added, seeing as The Cool Doods were standing right behind him.

Dirk gave his sort-of boss a nudge. 'You gonna treat me and Marge, Hec?' he smiled.

'Nope,' said Hector.

Dwayne pulled a pair of shiny metal tongs
out of a tub and pincered three donuts
onto a tray. 'Here you go,' he smiled,
passing the tray to Rhubarb.

Stuffed into the middle of each donut was
a see-through plastic ball - the sort that
pops in half. Inside each ball was a Donut
Hole Monster, floating in a tiny puddle's-
worth of green slime.

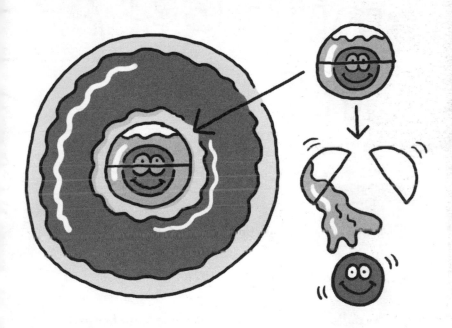

'They aren't in bags?' said Melvin,
his nose drooping.

'Erm, no, afraid not,' said Dwayne. He pushed his cap a centimetre up his forehead. 'I just thought, you know, nobody wants bags these days, do they?'

Rhubarb sniffed the air.

'What is it, Rubes?' said Yoshi. 'You smell a mystery?'

'I'm not sure,' said Rhubarb, staring into Dwayne's eyes. 'Something about the way he talked about those bags . . .'

Yoshi pulled his notepad out. 'The Mystery Of The Way Dwayne From Donut Diner Talked About Those Bags,' he said, reading out what he was writing.

Rhubarb whipped a business card out of her pocket. 'Rhubarb Plonsky,' she said, handing it to Dwayne. 'Editor of The Daily Donut.'

Rhubarb Plonsky
Editor, The Daily Donut

All Mysteries Investigat

Dwayne looked at Rhubarb's card.
'All Mysteries Investigated,' he said, reading the bit at the bottom. 'Well I can assure you there are no mysteries to be investi-'

A STRANGE RUMBLING SOUND ECHOED OUTSIDE THE BUILDING.

'Strange,' said Dwayne. 'That's been happening ever since the storm the other night.'

'Come on, let's go sit down,' said Rhubarb to Yoshi and Melvin.

Yoshi stuffed his notepad into his pocket and followed her, plonking his bum on the squishy orange seat.

Rhubarb picked up her donut. 'I've got my eye on that Dwayne character,' she said, poking her finger through the hole, and the plastic ball bounced onto the table.

The offer

Rhubarb popped her ball open and fished a Donut Hole Monster out of the green slime. 'Ooh, gold!' she said, as The Cool Doods sat down in the booth next to them.

'That's a super-rare one!' called Dwayne from behind his counter.

Yoshi held his ball up. 'I got yellow!' he smiled, peering through the snotty gunk at the creature inside.

Melvin looked down at his free toy. It was still floating in its ball, but he could already see the colour. 'Blue,' he said, wishing was hidden inside a packet.

Rhubarb pulled her torch out of her rucksack and pumped the handle, shining the bulb into her little monster's eyes. 'Don't glow much, do they?' she muttered, cupping it in her hands to see if that made any difference.

Melvin took a bite of his donut. 'This is why I don't open toy bags,' he said. 'They're always a let-down.'

Lying on the table was a shiny little leaflet with every single one of the Donut Hole Monsters lined up on it. There were fifty to collect, each of them a slightly different colour.

'Mine's green!' said Hector's voice from the table next door.

'Hey Plonsky,' said Dirk, sticking his head over the wall that divided the two booths. 'I'll have yours if you don't want it.'

'In your dreams, Measles,' snapped Rhubarb. 'I'm keeping this for research purposes.'

Hector appeared next to Dirk, sucking on a Donut Diner cup filled with cola.

'Tell you what, why don't I take care of yours?' he said, snatching the Donut Hole Monster out of Dirk's hand and clicking his fingers. 'Yours too, Marge.'

SLURP!

Dor
Dir

Marjorie blinked. 'No way!' she said. 'It's mine.'

Hector turned his head round to face her. 'Do you like being a Cool Dood, Pinecone?' he asked, and she frowned, passing him her toy.

'Now, how much do you want for your ones?' asked Hector, twizzling his head back round to face the Daily Donut Club.

Yoshi looked at his. 'Five pounds,' he said.

'10p,'

said Hector.

'NO THANKS,'

said Yoshi.

'Alright then, 20p,'

said Hector.

Yoshi shook his head as Melvin peered down at his Donut Hole Monster. It wasn't like he wanted it all that much, anyway. I mean, it wasn't even in a bag, was it?

Rhubarb squidged herself out of the booth. 'Think I might go investigate that rumbling noise,' she said. 'You two coming?'

Yoshi jumped up and followed her to the door while Melvin stayed in his seat, looking from the Daily Donut gang to the Cool Doods.

Hector took a sip of his cola. 'Hey Pebbles,' he said. 'I've got a question for you.'

Melvin glanced up. 'Yeah?' he said.

'Yeah,' smiled Hector, nodding at the brand new blue Donut Hole Monster in Melvin's hand. 'How do you fancy a trial membership of The Cool Doods?'

Melvin's wee

Suddenly there was a knock on the window. Melvin looked round and saw Rhubarb and Yoshi on the other side of it.

'You coming or what?' mouthed Rhubarb.

'In a minute,' said Melvin, and Rhubarb and Yoshi wandered off in the direction of the old hole.

Dirk nudged his sort-of boss. 'What are you doing, Hec?' he said. 'There's no room for another Dood in the gang.'

Hector pointed at the seat next to Marjorie. 'What about there?' he said, and Melvin pictured himself plonking his bum down in it.

Hector inspected his nails. 'So what's it gonna be, Pebbles?' he asked.

Melvin stood up and walked round to The Cool Doods' booth. He placed his Donut Hole Monster on the table, in front of Hector. 'You've got a deal,' he said.

'I knew you'd come around,' smiled Hector, picking it up. He finished off his cola, popped all four of his plastic balls open and poured the slime-covered creatures into the empty cup.

The green gunk melted together and the lumps of plastic floated towards each other. The light above shone down on them and for a millisecond, Melvin could've sworn their eyes started to glow.

He rubbed his own eyes and looked again, but the monsters just stared up at him, their eyeballs back to boring old normal.

'Mind if I sit down?' he said, pointing at the seat next to Marge.

Hector smiled up from his cup. 'Actually, Pebbles,' he said, 'the trial starts Monday.'

'Oh yeah, of course,' said Melvin, turning round. 'I'll see you then, then.'

'Toodle-oo,' called Marjorie as he headed out of Donut Diner and caught up with Rhubarb and Yoshi by the fence that went round the old hole.

'Where've you been?' asked Rhubarb.

Melvin scratched his bum. 'Oh, erm, I needed a wee,' he said all quickly. 'A really long one. So . . . what about this crack, then?'

Yoshi rattled the fence. 'Can't get any closer than this,' he said.

Rhubarb sniffed the air. 'Funny old pong coming out of it, though,' she said.

Yoshi whipped his notepad out.

'The Strange Case Of The Stinky Smell Coming Out Of The Crack In The Old Hole,'

he said, writing it down at the same time.

'Catchy,' said Melvin, wondering how many seconds it was until Monday morning.

Melvin the Cool Dood

Melvin stayed home all Saturday, arranging his toy packets in his bedroom and daydreaming about becoming a Cool Dood.

? ? ?

RIS

Mystery Toy!

'Why don't you go out with your friends, Melv,' said his dad at breakfast on Sunday morning.

'Nah, I'm too busy,' said Melvin.

'What, dusting your toy bags?' laughed Violet.

Melvin glared at his sister. 'I dusted them yesterday, actually,' he said.

After that he went upstairs and laid on his bed, memorising the Cool Rools for the next day.

TOY PACKETS RULE!

Hokum City

113

'Melv!' cried Rhubarb, catching up with him at the school gates on Monday morning. 'I've been looking for you.'

'Oh yeah?' said Melvin, peering around for Hector.

Everywhere he looked, kids were holding Donut Hole Monsters. Some of them had more than one, and a few were carrying their collections around in Donut Diner cups.

'I wanted to check you're still on for my talk at the town hall tomorrow night,' said Rhubarb. 'Yoshi's staying at mine after if you wanna join us?'

Melvin nodded. 'Sounds great,' he said.
'Listen, I really need a wee. Mind if
I scoot off?'

'You and your wees!' chuckled Rhubarb,
spotting Yoshi walking through the gates.
'Ooh, there's Fujikawa. I'll go tell him you're
staying tomorrow night. He'll be so pleased!'

Rhubarb wandered off and Melvin strolled
up to Dirk and Marge. 'Either of you seen
Hector?' he asked.

'Who wants to know?' asked Dirk. He was
holding a brand new spotty purple and
green Donut Hole Monster in his hand.

Marge was flicking through a magazine. 'He's down Donut Diner having a breakfast donut,' she said, not looking up.

'Delicious it was too,' said Hector, appearing behind Melvin. His Donut Diner cup was half-full of slime now. Floating around in it were seven Donut Hole Monsters. 'I see you've got a new one, Dirk,' he smiled. 'Hand it over.'

'But I already gave you one,' said Dirk, peering down at his spotty lump of plastic.

'You know the rules, Measles,' smiled Hector, snatching it out of his hand.

Hector cracked the ball open like an egg and poured the slimy Donut Hole Monster into his cup. He held it up and peered in, the dots in his eyes looking like they'd doubled in size.

He turned to Melvin. 'How's it feel to officially be a Cool Dood, Pebbles?' he smiled.

Marjorie licked a finger and turned a page of her magazine. 'Temporarily, of course,' she said.

Hector blinked and his eyes went back to normal. 'Of course,' he said. 'By the way, we're having a little sleepover at Measles's house tomorrow night.'

'Yeah, and Pebble's not invited!' snapped Dirk.

Melvin itched his earlobe. 'I'm not sure I can go to a sleepover on a school night anyway,' he said. 'I mean, I'd be totally cool with it, my parents are just really square. I'm not, I'm completely round.'

'Let's see what Mr and Mrs Pebble say, shall we?' smiled Hector, holding up a fist, and Melvin high-fived it, then realised he was supposed to be bumping it, so closed his hand, giving it a sort of cuddle with his palm instead.

'One more thing,' said Hector.

'Anything,' said Melvin.

Hector tapped his lips. 'Rhubarb's Donut Hole Monster,' he said.

'The gold one?' said Melvin.

'It's super rare,' said Hector. 'Do you think it could . . . disappear, maybe?'

'Disappear?' said Melvin. 'I don't think so. I mean, its eyes are sposed to glow in the dark, but go completely see-through? I doubt it could do that.'

Hector smiled. 'Very funny,' he chuckled. Then he stopped smiling and stared into Melvin's eyes. 'Do I really have to explain myself?'

Dirk nudged Melvin. 'He wants you to steal it off her, stupid,' he said.

Melvin gulped. 'Oh right,' he said.

'She doesn't even like the thing,' said Hector. 'You'd be doing her a favour.'

He gave his Donut Diner cup a jiggle and the little monsters bobbed around inside.

'I'll see what I can do,' said Melvin, heading towards the classroom, now officially a trial member of The Cool Doods.

Trouser pocket

The rest of Melvin's day was spent hanging out with Rhubarb and Yoshi, secretly smiling over at Hector and The Cool Doods whenever he got the chance.

'Hey Rhubarb, let's have a look at your Donut Hole Monster,' he said at lunch, when they were standing under the big tree by the library.

She whipped it out of her pocket and handed it over. 'Bit weird how everyone's so into them, don't you think?' she said, as Melvin pretended to study it.

A kid walked past holding a cup
with three Donut Hole Monsters
floating in it. He was grinning
from ear to ear and the dots in
his eyes were all big, like Hector's.

'That's what happens with these sorts of toys,'
said Melvin, trying to work out how he was
going to sneak her one into his pocket. 'People
get obsessed.'

Rhubarb nodded. 'Yeah I spose,' she said.
'Not us, though, eh.'

'No, we're too into mysteries!' smiled Yoshi.

'And Melvin only likes toys that are in bags,' smiled Rhubarb.

'Oops!' cried Melvin, pretending to drop Rhubarb's monster. He slipped it into his trouser pocket. 'Oh no, I've lost your Donut Hole Monster, Rubes!' he said, peering around on the ground. 'It's ... it's completely disappeared.'

Yoshi pointed at Melvin's pocket. 'It's in your pocket, Melv,' he said.

He turned to Rhubarb. 'It fell straight into his trouser pocket! In all my years investigating mysteries, I've never seen something fall into a trouser pocket by accident like that.'

Melvin laughed. 'You haven't?' he said.
'Things are falling into my pockets all
the time!'

'But a TROUSER pocket?' said Yoshi.
'They're so tight.'

'Guess I'm just lucky when it comes to
dropping things,' said Melvin. 'Maybe
I should hold on to this one for you, Rubes.'

Rhubarb plucked the Donut Hole Monster
out of Melvin's fingers. 'Oh, I never drop
stuff,' she said. 'It's my
middle name!'

Melvin sighed. 'Okay,' he said.

'Perhaps you should look after mine though,
Melv,' said Yoshi. 'I'm a bit of a dropper if
I'm being honest with you.'

He went to drop his toy into Melvin's hand, then paused. 'That's weird,' he said. 'My fingers won't let go.'

'Let me help you,' said Melvin, snatching Yoshi's monster and holding it up so that Hector, who'd been watching from the bench across the playground, could see.

Hector gave him a thumbs-up. 'And the gold one, Pebbles,' he mouthed.

'I'll try again later,' mouthed Melvin back.

'I still don't see how it fell into your pocket,' said Yoshi.

Shiny little Pebbles

'Wanna follow me home from a distance?' said a familiar voice from behind Melvin as he strolled out the gates at half past three.

He'd left the classroom in a hurry, excited to get home and ask his mum and dad about Dirk's sleepover.

'Hi, Vi,' he said, turning round to see his sister wheeling her bike. 'Good day?'

'Oh yeah, the best,' said Violet, taking off her rucksack and slinging it into the basket on the front.

Melvin spotted a couple of older girls, about Violet's age, strolling past, coming from the direction of Donut High School.

'Hey newbie,' one of them called to Violet. 'Hanging out with the kiddywinkles, I see.'

Violet turned away from them. 'So, how's it going with The Cool Doods?' she asked, and Melvin wondered if she maybe hadn't had such a great day after all.

'Good, actually,' smiled Melvin. 'They're giving me a trial membership.'

Violet chuckled. 'Ooh, a trial membership, how exciting,' she said, sounding a bit more like her old self again, and Melvin gave her a nudge, which is sort of like a tiny little hug if the person you're giving it to is your sister.

'How was school, my shiny little Pebbles?' smiled their mum fifteen minutes later, as they walked through their front door.

'Amazing!' beamed Melvin. 'I've been invited to a sleepover with The Cool Doods!'

Norman patted his son on the head like he was a dog. 'That sounds fun,' he said. 'When is it, Friday night, Saturday?'

'Actually it's tomorrow,' said Melvin. 'I told them you'd be cool with it, what with you being the best parents in the whole wide world and everything.'

'Hmmm, I'm not sure about that, Melvin,' said his mum, arranging her empty jam jars on the kitchen shelf. 'I do love an empty jam jar,' she cooed.

Violet, who was peering down at her phone, grinned. 'Nice try, Melv,' she said.

'Oh, but that's not fair,' groaned Melvin. 'I mean, you're the ones who dragged me to stupid old Donut Island, away from my best friends in Hokum City. And now you're stopping me from making new ones?'

'Hang on a millisecond,' said Violet. 'I thought you said your old friends were a bunch of losers?'

Melvin did his shocked face.

"Only cos you said it first!"

he cried.

'Melvin's right, Vi,' said his dad.

'Fair enough,' said Violet, heading upstairs. 'But you'd never let me go to a sleepover at his age.'

Norman held his hands up. 'Nobody's saying he's going to the sleepover,' he said.

'But you ruined my life!'

wailed Melvin, dropping to his knees.

'I'm sure you'll survive,' said his mum.

Melvin lay on the floor, trying to come up with another idea. Then he remembered Rhubarb's talk.

'Scrap Dirk's sleepover,' he said, springing to his feet. 'I completely forgot - Rhubarb's doing a talk down at Donut Town Hall tomorrow night.'

'Now that's more like it,' said Norman. 'I do like Rhubarb, she's such a sensible girl.'

'Yes, she is,' said Melvin. 'Thing is, she invited me to stay over at hers afterwards, and I'd so hate to let her down.'

Deirdre stroked her chin, half looking at her display of jam jars. 'Well, if it's only next door,' she said.

'See, I knew you two were the best!' cried Melvin, leaping up the stairs to his bedroom.

Melvin's room

Melvin bounded into his room and strolled over to the shelves where he'd lined up his toy packets.

'Hello my little beauties,' he said, picking up a Hokum City Hotdogs one. He could still remember getting it back in his home town a few years ago. 'So much better than a Donut Hole Monster.'

He smiled, giving it a fiddle and trying to work out what was inside.

'Seriously, what is it with you and those blimming packets,' said Violet, pushing open the door.

'I dunno,' said Melvin. 'I just like them.'

Violet wandered over and picked one up. 'What'd happen if I ripped this open right now?' she said, pincering its crimped seal in her fingertips.

BLURGS

THEY PUKE →

'NO!' cried Melvin. 'Just leave it, Vi.'

'Toys are made for playing with, Melvin,' she said.

'I know,' he sighed, pulling Yoshi's yellow Donut Hole Monster out of his pocket. He hadn't had a chance to give it to Hector yet.

'A toy with no bag?' gasped Violet. 'Quick, get it out of the house!'

Melvin giggled. 'It's not mine,' he said, feeling a bit guilty. 'It's Yoshi's. Well it's Hector Frisbee's now, actually. He's the leader of The Cool Doods, you know.'

'Sounds complicated,' said Violet.

'Yeah I spose it is,' said Melvin.

135

His sister looked at him. 'You and those blooming Cool Doods,' she said. 'You're better off with Rhubarb and Yoshi by the sounds of it, Melv.'

'The Cool Doods are alright,' said Melvin.

Violet shrugged. 'I dunno,' she said. 'They sound a bit . . . well, a bit like your toy bags, actually.'

'What do you mean?' said Melvin.

Violet looked at the one she was holding. 'Once you've seen what's inside, all the excitement's gone,' she said, chucking it on the floor and walking out the room.

Melvin picked it up and placed it carefully on the shelf.

'She doesn't know what she's talking about,' he said, stuffing Yoshi's Donut Hole Monster back into his pocket.

Great Aunt Pebble

Next it was Tuesday, which Melvin wanted to get through as quickly as possible, seeing as it was the big sleepover at Dirk's house that night.

'You alright, Melv?' asked Yoshi. He and Rhubarb had been talking about **The Strange Case Of The Stinky Smell Coming Out Of The Crack In The Old Hole** for the whole of lunch. 'You haven't said a word all day.'

'Huh?' said Melvin. He'd been wondering how he was going to steal Rhubarb's Donut Hole Monster.

Rhubarb peered out of the canteen window.
'Check out that sky,' she said, and Melvin
looked up. A strange purple mist was swirling
above the trees and buildings.

A freckly girl walked past with a Donut Diner
cup filled with Donut Hole Monsters. 'I swear
there's something up with those toys,' said
Yoshi. 'It's like they put people in a trance or
something.'

'Maybe it's all linked,' said Rhubarb, still staring
out the window.

'What's all linked?' asked Yoshi.

'EVERYTHING,' said Rhubarb. 'That smell coming out of the crack in the hole, the purple clouds, the Donut Hole Monsters making people act all weird . . .'

Melvin laughed. 'Not everything's one of your little mysteries, Rubes,' he said.

Rhubarb shrugged. 'Oh by the way, hope you're both looking forward to the sleepover. My mum's cooking her special - Chicken Kiev and chips!'

'Sleepover?' said Melvin, thinking she was talking about the one round Dirk's.

Rhubarb tapped Melvin's head. 'Wake up, Pebbles,' she said. 'It's my big talk tonight, remember?'

'We won't let you down, Rubes.' Yoshi smiled.

'Thanks, Yosh,' said Rhubarb. 'Melv, you're coming, right?'

Melvin blinked. 'Erm,' he said, scrabbling around inside his brain for an excuse. 'I'm, er . . . my dad's great aunt's coming over for dinner. It's a last-minute thing, haven't seen her for years. Really sorry, Rhubarb.'

'Oh right,' said Rhubarb, her nose drooping.
Then it started to sniff, almost like she
wasn't in charge of the thing.

'What is it, Rubes?' asked Yoshi.

Rhubarb's eyes crossed as she peered down
at her nose. 'This great aunt of yours,
Melv - what's her name?'

Melvin squirmed in his seat. 'Great Aunt . . .
Pebble?' he said.

'How old is she?' asked Rhubarb.

'A hundred-and-twenty-nine,' said Melvin,
immediately realising that was way too old.
'I mean thirty-two. No, eighty-five.'

Yoshi blinked. 'Doesn't sound like you
know her very well,' he said.

The Cool Doods scraped out of their chairs
and headed towards the Daily Donut table.
Hector, who was now carrying an extra-large
Donut Diner cup, snatched an orange monster
toy out of a little
girl's hand as
he passed her.
'I'll have that,
thank you
very much,'
he said.

Donut
Diner

They got to Melvin, Rhubarb and Yoshi
and stopped. 'Ah, Pebbles, looking forward
to this evening?' smiled Hector.

Melvin gulped. 'Oh yes, I haven't seen Great Aunt Pebble in years!' he said, turning to Rhubarb. 'I was telling Hector about Great Aunt Pebble earlier. He's got a great aunt too, haven't you, Hector?'

Hector looked confused for a second, then nodded. 'Oh yeah, that's right,' he said, winking at Melvin. 'Great Aunt Frisbee. She's the best.'

'Great aunts are so great,' said Melvin, smiling round at everyone. 'You should get one, Rubes.'

Rhubarb looked at Hector, then at Melvin. 'I'll see if Donut Supermarket have any,' she said, as the bell for afternoon lessons clanged.

The sleep-over

You know how time keeps jumping forward with each new chapter? Well now it was Tuesday night and Melvin was round Dirk Measles's house with Hector and Marge.

He'd already met Dirk's mum and dad, and Dirk had introduced Melvin by saying, 'This is that loser from class I told you about.'

Then he'd eaten his dinner of fish fingers, chips and peas, which Dirk hadn't allowed him any tomato sauce with, saying, 'Only real-life Cool Doods get ketchup in this house.'

After that, he'd watched TV for about three hours, sitting on the little foot stool the whole way through because Dirk had said, 'You don't deserve to sit on the sofa yet.'

And now they were all in Dirk's bedroom, getting ready for bed.

Hector was sitting on Dirk's sofa bed holding his extra-large Donut Diner cup, a million monster toys floating around inside. Well not a million exactly, but quite a lot.

'Okay, Cool Doods,' he said, clicking his fingers. 'You know the rules - hand the toys over. One each, please.'

Dirk went over to a chest of drawers and opened the top one, pulling out a plastic ball with a beige Donut Hole Monster inside.

'This collection of yours is costing me a fortune,' he said, chucking it to Hector, who caught it in one hand and cracked it into his cup.

The green slime gurgled as the monster sank. The smile on its face turned into a frown. 'Hey, I didn't know they did that,' said Melvin.

'Did what?' said Hector, looking distracted. He ran his hand through his hair. The dots in his eyes had gone big again, and his face was kind of pale. 'Marjorie!' he barked. 'Donut Hole Monster!'

Marge scrabbled around in her bag and pulled out a plastic ball. 'Had to nick it off a first year,' she said, throwing it to him.

Hector caught it and peered through the slime. 'PINK?' he boomed, whipping a scrunched-up Donut Hole Monsters leaflet out of his pocket. 'I already have a pink one!' he said, pointing at a crossed-out one on his flyer.

He threw Marge's ball across the room and the slime splattered onto the wall. 'More!' he shouted.

'I NEED MORE!'

Melvin pulled Yoshi's yellow monster out of his rucksack and handed it shakily to Hector, who plopped it into his cup. This one's smile turned into a grimace too.

'Did you see that?' said Melvin. 'It's SO coool!'

'SO coool!' said Marjorie, copying the way he'd just said it, and Dirk chuckled.

'Sorry,' said Melvin, even though he wasn't sure what he'd done wrong.

'Sorry,' squeaked Dirk in a loserish voice, and Marge laughed.

Melvin's nose drooped. This wasn't like the sleepovers he'd had with his friends back in Hokum City at all. 'Hey, I know! Shall we play a game?' he said, trying to perk it up a bit.

THE COOL DOODS'
COOL ROOLS

1. Reading is for losers
2. No talking to Daily Donut losers
3. Never get excited
4. Check hair a lot
5. Walk like you can't be bothered
6. Memorise The Cool Rools
7. No playing games
8. Yawn when person talking to you
9. Turn page over for more...

'Er, I don't think so,' said Marge. She pointed at the wall, where Dirk had a copy of the Cool Rools pinned up. Number seven was 'No playing games'.

Dirk looked over at Hector and smiled to himself. 'Hey Melvin, whatever happened with that gold Donut Hole Monster of Rhubarb's?' he asked, all innocently.

Hector's head snapped up and he stared at Melvin. His eyes looked almost like they were glowing. 'Yes, Pebbles,' he said in deep, growly voice,

'WHERE IS MY GOLD ONE?'

Weird Hector

'I- I'm working on it, Heck,' said Melvin, starting to panic. 'I'll get it soon, I promise!'

Hector blinked. His eyes went back to normal. 'There's a good boy,' he said in his regular voice.

Melvin breathed a sigh of relief as Hector peered down at his cup. 'I have thirty-four Donut Hole Monsters now,' he said, his left eyelid twitching. 'Not bad, I suppose. **BUT NOT GREAT**. That's sixteen more to get. And I need that gold one, Pebbles. I need it

«VERY BADLY.»

Hector held his giant cup in front of his
face and started to laugh, the little
monsters jiggling around inside. Melvin
peered at him through the green slime.
He looked like a bit of a monster himself.

Dirk stared at his sort-of boss. 'Time for
bed, I think,' he said, switching off the light
and disappearing under his duvet. 'Night
Hector, night Marge,' he mumbled, leaving
Melvin out.

'Night Doods,' said Melvin, lying on his back
and staring up at the ceiling. It was covered
in glow-in-the-dark stars, but they weren't
glowing very much.

That's how Melvin felt right now - only
half charged-up.

153

Outside, the sky was purple and the moon was almost full. The window was ajar and stinky purple air floated through it, straight up Melvin's nostrils.

'Maybe it's all linked,'

said Rhubarb's voice inside his head.

He peered over at Hector. The monster toys were definitely doing something strange to him. But how did that link to those weird clouds and the horrible smelly air?

Melvin must've been lying there thinking about all that for quite a while, because the next time he looked around it was dark and The Cool Doods were asleep, snoring their heads off.

Apart from Hector, that is.

He was sitting up in bed now. All thirty-four of his Donut Hole Monsters were jostling around in the plastic cup like bubbles trying to escape from a fizzy drink.

A strange whispering sound drifted up from the toys, like a crowd of people's voices screeching out of a phone.

Outside, the moon was shining extra-bright. A wisp of purple cloud drifted through the open window and hovered around Hector's head like an evil thought bubble. His eyes opened wide and started to glow.

Melvin gasped as Hector stood up and walked across the room. He stopped at the chest of drawers and opened the top one, reaching his hand in and pulling out three small, plastic balls.

'Cheeky old Measles,' muttered Melvin to himself. 'He's been hiding them away!'

Hector carried the balls back to his cup and plopped the monsters in, then slid under his duvet and closed his eyes.

Melvin wriggled deep into his sleeping bag. Inside it was pitch black and he could hear his heart beating.

"This is a job for The Daily Donut Club,"

he whispered to himself, wondering if he was ever going to get to sleep.

Rubbish morning

Melvin was tired as he walked to school with The Cool Doods the next morning, purple clouds still swirling in the sky.

'Poo, what's that STINK?' said Dirk, as they strolled towards the gates of Donut Juniors. 'The whole town smells like a giant rubbish bin!'

The playground was filled with kids holding
Donut Diner cups, green slime and evil-looking
monster toys sloshing around inside.

A girl walked past with her hair sticking up like
she'd been struck by lightning. Her eyes-dots
were the size of conkers and her collection of
bobbling beasts whispered like a million grannies,
shrunk to the size of fleas.

Melvin spotted Rhubarb and Yoshi standing
under the big tree. 'You'll never guess what
happened!' he cried, running towards them.

'Morning, Melvin,' said Rhubarb. She didn't
look like she'd slept very well either.

'It's the Donut Hole Monsters,' panted Melvin, getting his breath back. 'You were right - they're doing something super weird to the kids!'

'No kidding,' said Rhubarb, looking at all the boys and girls walking around with their cups. 'How was your Great Aunt Pebble, by the way?'

'Fantastic. Never Better,' said Melvin. 'Forget about her though, it's the Donut Hole Monsters we need to worry about.'

Yoshi pushed his glasses up his nose. 'What happened, Melv?' he asked.

Melvin paused. How was he going to explain about Hector and the purple cloud without telling them he'd gone round Dirk's the night before?

'I-I can't tell you,' mumbled Melvin. 'But I think it's all linked - just like you said.'

Hector strolled up with The Cool Doods. 'The gold one, Pebbles,' he whispered into Melvin's ear as he went past.

"I REALLY
want that
gold one..."

Melvin thought back to Hector zombie-ing around Dirk's bedroom the night before. It was probably a good idea to keep on his good side for now.

'I think I should look after your monster toy,
Rubes,' he said. 'Just to keep it safe.'

Yoshi nudged Melvin before Rhubarb could
answer. 'That reminds me, Melv,' he said.
'Could I see my yellow one for a second?
Over here by the tree trunk, maybe.'

Oh great, thought Melvin, following Yoshi.
Now what am I gonna do?

'It's not really about my Donut Hole Monster,'
said Yoshi, once they were far away enough
from Rhubarb that she couldn't hear.

Melvin relaxed. 'What is it then, Yosh?'

Yoshi kicked a twig. 'It's a real shame you didn't come to Rhubarb's talk last night,' he said.

'Oh that,' said Melvin. 'Well, you know, Great Aunt Pebble and everything . . .'

'Me and Mrs Plonsky were the only ones there,' said Yoshi. 'It was awful. Rhubarb's pretending it's all fine, but I think she's really upset.'

Melvin's nose drooped. 'Poor old Rhubarb,' he said, as the noise of somebody shouting echoed down his earholes.

Rhubarb's present

'Oi, Pinecone!' shouted the voice, and Melvin twizzled round.

An older-looking girl holding a half-full Donut Diner cup was standing next to a younger-looking boy. 'My brother says you nicked his Donut Hole Monster,' said the girl to Marge. 'Pink one, it was.'

Marjorie scoffed. 'As if!' she laughed. 'Everyone knows Cool Rool number eleven – No Collecting Donut Hole Monsters.'

'Whatever,' said the girl. 'Just give it back.'

Hector stared at the Donut Diner cup in the girl's hand. Then he reached his arm out and grabbed it.

'Hey, what are you doing?' cried the girl.

Hector's hair shot up, like he'd been plugged into a socket or something.

'GIVE THEM TO ME!' he boomed.

The girl's hand opened and she staggered backwards. Hector poured her monster toys into his half-full cup and smiled.

'Forty-four!' he cackled, counting up his collection at super-freaky speed.

'Only six more to go, boss!' said Dirk.

Hector whipped his Donut Hole Monsters leaflet out of his pocket and started crossing off the ones he'd just stolen. 'The gold one, Pebbles,' he said, looking up at Melvin.

"I still need Rhubarb's gold one."

Rhubarb looked over at Melvin, confused. 'Wait a millisecond,' she said. 'Is that why you wanted to look after it?'

'No!' cried Melvin, walking back to her.

'Oops, looks like Melvin's in trouble with his girlfriend,' chuckled Marge.

'She is NOT my girlfriend!' snapped Melvin.

'That's not what you were whispering in your sleep last night,' chuckled Dirk. 'Ooh Rhubarb, I love you,' he cooed, doing his Melvin Pebble impression.

'That's a lie!' cried Melvin.

'Last night?' said Yoshi. 'What happened last night?'

Dirk yawned. 'We had the pleasure of Melvin's company round my house, didn't we, Doods?'

Rhubarb stuffed her hands in her pockets. 'Oh,' she said. 'I see.'

'It's not what you think, Rubes,' said Melvin, even though it completely was.

A kid walked past carrying a full-up Donut Diner cup. 'That looks promising,' said Hector, running after him with Dirk and Marge following behind.

Rhubarb pulled something out of her pocket. It was the size of a toy packet, but kind of homemade-looking. 'This was for you,' she said, passing it to Melvin.

Melvin took the little package and gave it a fiddle. 'What is it?' he said, feeling something round inside.

'Read the front,' said Yoshi.

Melvin looked down at the packet.

Donut Hole
Monster

SUPER RARE
GOLD EDITION!

'But that's your one, Rhubarb,' said Melvin.

Rhubarb shrugged. 'I just thought you really wanted it,' she said. 'I spose you may as well keep it now.'

Melvin opened his mouth as the bell for morning lessons started to clang.

Which was lucky for him, because he didn't know what to say.

The mystery of the Donut Hole Monsters

By the end of school, the air stank worse than ever and the sky was completely purple.

'Hurry home now, kids,' called Mr Thursday, as Melvin spotted Rhubarb and Yoshi walking towards Donut High Street.

'Talk about a mystery, eh?' Melvin said, pointing up at the clouds.

Rhubarb shrugged. 'Yeah,' she said.

'So . . .' he said. 'Fancy investigating it?'

Rhubarb shook her head. 'Think I'll just head home,' she said. 'I'm not really in the mood for mysteries today.'

'Me neither,' said Yoshi.

'Oh right,' said Melvin. 'I'll see you tomorrow, then?'

'I guess,' said Rhubarb, as she and Yoshi disappeared round the corner.

The Cool Doods wandered up to Melvin. Hector's hair was zig-zagging out of his head like millions of tiny lightning bolts.

'WHERE'S PLONSKY?' he boomed.

Melvin sighed. 'She went home,' he said.

'HOME?!' shrieked Hector.

'There, there, Hector,' said Dirk. 'We'll sort this out.'

He turned to Melvin. 'Hector's got forty-six Donut Hole Monsters now,' he said, pointing at the little toys swishing around in his cup. 'He's doing ever so well, aren't you boss?'

Hector growled, and for a millisecond it looked like his eyeballs were glowing.

'But he really needs that gold one, Melv,' said Marge, sounding a teeny-weeny bit scared.

Melvin cupped his hand round the little homemade bag in his pocket. 'Oh well,' he said. 'I'm sure he'll survive.'

'I–I don't think you understand, Melvin,' said Dirk. He nodded at Hector, whose forehead was twitching like an ant motorway had opened up underneath the skin. 'We have to complete his collection.'

Melvin scratched his bum, wondering what to do. He didn't really care about Hector's collection any more. He'd rather be hanging out with Rhubarb and Yoshi. But they weren't speaking to him.

If only he knew how to make it up to them.

Melvin stared at Hector, standing there with his extra-large Donut Diner cup. The Donut Hole Monsters bobbed around inside, whispering to their owner while purple clouds swirled behind him.

And that's when he had an idea.

'That's it,' he said. 'If Rhubarb and Yoshi can't solve The Mysterious Case Of The Donut Hole Monsters, I'll crack it for them!'

Dirk prodded Melvin. 'So are you gonna help us or what, Pebbles?' he asked.

Melvin smiled at The Cool Doods.

'Do you like mysteries?'

he asked.

Dirk and Marjorie shrugged. Hector grinned down at his monsters.

'Then follow me,' said Melvin, starting to run towards Donut Diner.

Super moon

Melvin and The Cool Doods sprinted the whole way to Donut Diner, the stink getting smellier with every step.

When they reached the building, Melvin gasped. Purple smoke was billowing out of the giant lightning crack behind it and a strange noise was rumbling under the ground.

'The purple clouds,' gasped Melvin.
'They're coming from the old hole too.'

It was getting dark, and the moon shone
like a giant glow-in-the-dark eye. It was
full-sized now and hanging almost directly
over the crack.

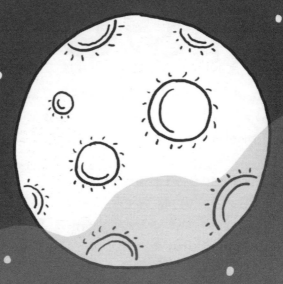

'That moon's ginormous,' said Dirk.

Marjorie nodded. 'It's a super moon,' she
said, not even trying to sound cool anymore.

Hector ignored them all. He marched up
to the door of Donut Diner and barged in.

Dwayne looked up. 'Ah Mr Frisbee, back so soon?' he said.

Everywhere Melvin looked, boys and girls were munching on donuts and popping open plastic balls.

Hector stomped over to the nearest kid and grabbed his cup, pouring the contents onto the floor. He dropped to his knees and started rummaging through the slime.

'YUMMY!' he roared, holding up a stripy yellow and blue lump of plastic.

'That's forty-seven now, Hector!' cried Dirk. 'You're getting there, Boss!'

Hector pulled his Donut Hole Monsters leaflet out of his pocket and crossed the one off he'd just got. 'THREE LEFT,' he growled.

The only ones that hadn't been scribbled over were light brown, silver and gold. 'FIND THEM,' Hector roared.

Marjorie and Dirk zoomed off, grabbing people's cups and stuffing their hands into the slime, pulling out the toys inside.

Melvin just stood and watched, his mouth hanging open. 'Super weird,' he whispered to himself.

Dirk ran up to Hector. 'Hector, Hector, I got one!' he cried, passing a lump of light brown plastic to his boss.

Hector plopped it into his cup as Marjorie appeared behind Dirk, holding another toy. 'I got the silver one!' she said, handing it to him.

He grabbed the little toy and held it up. 'THIS ISN'T SILVER!' he boomed.

Dirk nodded. 'Hector's right, Marge,' he said. 'It's grey.'

Marge's legs started to wobble. 'I'm s-s-sorry,' she stuttered.

'YOU ARE NOT A COOL DOOD!'

shrieked Hector, his eyeballs glowing.

'B-but I can try again,' said Marge. 'Please, give me another chance!'

Hector dropped the little grey monster on the floor as Dirk ran up to the counter and leapt over it.

'Employees only back here!' yelped Dwayne, but Dirk just ignored him. He ducked out of sight and reappeared, holding a large cardboard box.

'Hey, look what I've found!' he grinned, and everyone stopped to see.

'Free monsters!'

cried Dirk, tipping the box onto the counter. A million little plastic balls poured out, spilling over the floor of Donut Diner like evil marbles.

'Yahoo!' cried a pointy-nosed kid, diving into the sea of toys and starting to pop them open.

'Out of the way, losers!' shouted Dirk, jumping back over the counter and doing the same.

'Silver!' screamed another kid, picking up a ball. 'I've found a silver one!'

Marge whipped it out of his hand and threw it to Hector. 'Here you go, Boss,' she said. 'Can I be a Cool Dood again now?'

Hector caught the ball and cracked the silver monster into his cup. 'Forty-nine!' cried Dirk. 'Only the gold one left!'

Melvin gripped the little bag in his pocket as he watched the slime in Hector's cup start to bubble. The monsters inside whispered to Hector as his eyeballs shone.

'I've GOT to work out what's going on,'
muttered Melvin to himself.

Outside, the crack had got even bigger.
The ground seemed to be crumbling into it,
and the fence that went around the old
hole had completely collapsed.

Everyone in Donut Diner stared through the
window as a brownish kind of sludge rose up
from the earth, bubbling and sloshing like
a giant bolognese sauce.

'Everybody panic!' wailed Dwayne, and a million kids started running around, screaming and waggling their arms.

"THE GOLD ONE!"

boomed Hector.

"FIND THE GOLD ONE!"

Melvin started running towards the front door, but as he passed the empty cardboard box Dirk had tipped over, he spotted something lying at the bottom of it.

He skidded to a stop and reached in, pulling out a scrap of plastic. 'What's this?' he said. There was a big capital D written on it, but nothing else.

'W-what's happening?' said Dirk, staring out the window.

'I've no idea,' said Melvin, 'but I know a person who might.'

He stuffed the scrap of plastic into his pocket and headed towards the door, just in time to see it crash open.

Doodard and Doshi

Rhubarb and Yoshi barged through the door, pinching their noses.

'Melvin!' cried Rhubarb, except it came out as 'Delvin!' what with her pinching her nose and everything.

'Rhubarb!' said Melvin, running towards her. 'I thought you were going home!'

Rhubarb de-pinched her hooter. 'You know me and Yoshi,' she said. 'We can never resist a good mystery!'

Melvin laughed. 'I'm sorry, Rubes,' he said. 'I've been an idiot.'

'Forget about it,' said Rhubarb, pointing out of the window. 'We've got worse things to worry about.'

Outside, the entire circle of earth had disappeared and spurts of bolognese sauce were shooting out of what was now a giant hole.

'The giant hole,' cried Yoshi. 'It's reappeared!'

Melvin zoomed in on Rhubarb's hand. She was holding a bit of plastic. It was covered in mud and crinkled up like it'd been lying in a rubbish bin for a thousand years.

'Hey, what's that?' he asked.

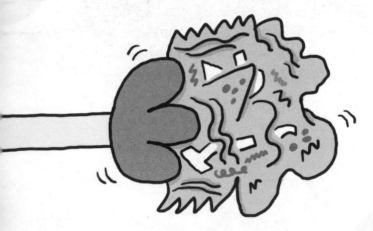

'I found it down by the hole,' said Rhubarb, holding it up.

It looked exactly like the bit Melvin had just found in the cardboard box, except bigger.

He pulled his piece out and held it next to hers. 'They fit together,' said Yoshi, and Melvin gasped.

It was a toy packet.

Yoshi scrunched his face up. 'Wait a minute, so the monster toys DID come in bags?' he said.

Rhubarb blinked. 'But why would somebody take them out of their bags?' she said.

They all looked at Dwayne.

'There's no time for that right now,' said Melvin. 'Let's just make sure Hector doesn't complete his collection. I've got a feeling something bad'll happen if he does!'

He stopped talking, feeling a strange sensation inside his trouser pocket all of a sudden. It was the sort of feeling you'd get if a Donut Hole Monster had just landed straight in it.

Except instead of a Donut Hole Monster, it felt more like a hand.

He twizzled his head round and came face to face with Hector.

Hector completes his collection

'GOT IT!' boomed Hector, holding up Melvin's toy packet - the paper one Rhubarb and Yoshi had made him.

Donut Hole Monster

SUPER RARE GOLD EDITION!

'Hey, that's mine!' cried Melvin, cried Melvin, reaching out to grab it back. But not fast enough.

Hector ripped the toy packet open.

"NOOO!"

screamed Melvin.

Hector stuffed his fingers into the bag and pulled out the plastic ball.

He cracked the ball open and plopped the lump of gold plastic into his cup.

"SUCCESS!"

he roared.

"MY COLLECTION IS COMPLETE!"

He held the cup above his head and the slime inside swished and swayed. Marge, who was cowering behind a bin with Dirk, pointed at the cup. 'W-what's going on in there?' she warbled.

Inside, a hundred little Donut Hole Monster eyes were glowing. 'Uh oh,' said Yoshi, stepping backwards. 'That doesn't look good.'

The slime in Hector's cup was frothing out the top of it now.

'What's it doing, Yosh?' yelped Melvin.

'I dunno,' said Yoshi. 'Some kind of chemical reaction I guess . . .'

'COOL!' smiled Hector.

Dirk peered over the top of his bin. 'Something about this feels very, very wrong,' he warbled.

'VERY, VERY RIGHT, YOU MEAN!' cackled Hector.

And that's exactly the millisecond the slime curled out the top of his cup and bit him straight on the nose.

"Danger at Donut Diner"

'Arrgghh!' screamed Hector, falling backwards and dropping his cup. He shook his head and his eyes clicked back to normal.
'That slime . . . it just bit me on the nose!'

Melvin pointed at Hector. 'Hey, he's back to normal,' he said.

Rhubarb nodded. 'The Donut Hole Monsters got what they wanted,' she said. 'They don't need him any more.'

'Got what they wanted?' said Yoshi.

'Somebody to complete their collection,' said Rhubarb.

Hector's cup rolled under a booth and out the other side, into the middle of Donut Diner.

'What's going on?' cried a kid from across the room as her cup of slime leapt out of her hand and headed towards Hector's.

Dwayne's head shot from left to right, watching as cup after cup flew out of hand after hand.

'The slime,' Dirk gasped. 'It's sticking together!'

Sure enough, the clumps of gooey gunk were slithering out of their cups and joining up with each other, creating one big ball of green jelly.

The giant bogey rose up, the glowing eyes of the Donut Hole Monsters inside swivelling around as if they were one.

'The toys,' cried Rhubarb. 'They're controlling the slime!'

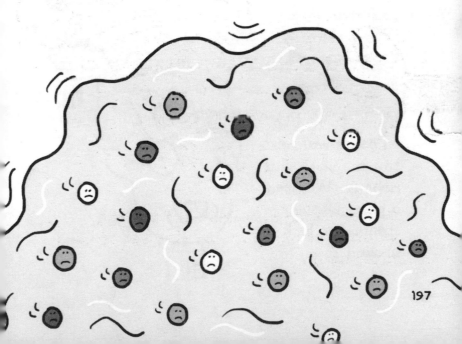

'I – I think it's headed this way,' stuttered Marjorie, grabbing Dirk's hand and running to the other side of the restaurant. 'Don't let it eat me,' she wailed, as Hector followed. 'I'm too cool to die!'

Yoshi turned to Rhubarb. 'We need a plan,' he said.

Rhubarb turned to Melvin. 'We need a plan,' she said as well.

Melvin turned to whoever was next to him, which was nobody. 'We need a plan,' he said, starting to look around.

"Melvin has" an "idea"

'How about something from behind the counter?' cried Rhubarb.

Dwayne clambered over it and popped back up holding a pair of donut tongs. 'These any good?' he asked.

Rhubarb shook her head. 'What we need is some kind of containment system,' she said.

Melvin looked down. He was still holding the mud-covered toy packet he and Rhubarb had found.

Across the room, Hector, Dirk and
Marjorie were squidged into a
booth with the giant slime
monster heading
towards them.

Dwayne had run over and was pincering at
it with his tongs.

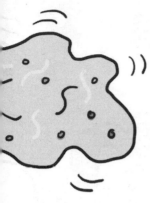

Melvin shook his head. 'This is why I don't open toy packets,' he said, picturing his collection, sitting on the shelf in his bedroom at home.

Then he thought of his mum, standing in the kitchen below, organising her empty jam jars.

Melvin clicked his fingers. 'Hey, I think I've just had an idea!' he smiled.

'The plan'

Melvin turned to Dwayne. 'Have you got a phone?' he yelled.

Dwayne stopped pincering the monster and twizzled round. 'Course I've got a blooming phone,' he said, whipping a mobile out of his pocket and holding it up all proudly.

'Can I borrow it?' asked Melvin.

'Here you go,' said Dwayne, chucking it across the room.

'Thanks,' said Melvin, as the great slimy green beast opened its mouth and swallowed Dwayne in one gulp.

Rhubarb screamed.

"IT'S EATEN DWAYNE!"
she wailed.

'Yikes,' said Melvin, catching the phone. He quickly dialled a number while looking at Dwayne, who was floating around inside the monster, his arms waggling in slow motion.

The phone rang a few times then somebody answered. 'Hello?' warbled a wobbly voice on the other end.

'Violet?' said Melvin. 'Is that you?'

'Ooh no dear,' said the voice. 'This is Noreen. Noreen Dingle.'

Melvin looked at the phone. 'Noreen Dingle?' he said, hanging up. 'Wrong number.'

just walked from lounge

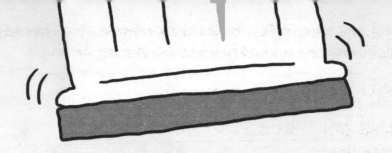

He tried again and this time Violet answered. 'Vi, I need your help,' said Melvin. 'Grab all Mum's jam jars and bring them down to Donut Diner!'

'Have you finally gone mad?' sighed his sister.

'There's no time to explain,' cried Melvin. 'It's an emergency!'

He hung up and peered over at The Cool Doods. They were still squidged into their booth. The only difference was that the wobbly mucus monster was now about a centimetre away from them.

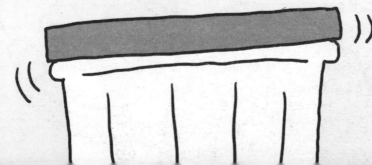

'Help me!' cried Hector, as the giant monster opened its gooey gob and swallowed all three of them up.

Yoshi yelped. 'Now it's gone and gobbled The Cool Doods!' he cried.

'What are we going to do?' said Rhubarb, watching as Hector, Dirk, Marge and Dwayne swam around inside the creature, surrounded by a million Donut Hole Monsters.

'We just have to wait,' said Melvin, hoping Violet wouldn't be too long.

"Get" "scooping"

Ten minutes later, Violet still wasn't there and things had changed a bit. The slime monster had slithered over to the door of the restaurant and blocked it with its fat green bum.

Melvin, Rhubarb and Yoshi were trapped inside the building. They were standing in front of the monster, holding a pair donut tongs each. Behind them cowered a crowd of petrified kids.

There was a screeching noise from outside.

'OI, GET AWAY FROM MY BROTHER, YOU BIG BULLY!'

bellowed Violet, screeching to a stop outside.

Melvin peered through the window of Donut Diner and spotted a cardboard box full of jam jars balanced inside her basket.

The monster toys inside the wobbly beast swivelled to face her and the enormous mouth smacked shut. The giant jelly collapsed into a huge green puddle, then rose up again on the other side of the restaurant. The big ball of slime started to herd the kids out the door of Donut Diner.

'MUMMY!' wailed a ginger-haired girl, making a run for it, and a wobbly green arm shot out of the monster, dragging her back into the crowd.

'Now what?' said Yoshi, tiptoeing backwards, away from the giant jelly but towards the massive hole.

Melvin pointed at the cardboard box in Violet's bike basket. 'Chuck me a few of those jam jars, Vi,' he called to her.

Violet wheeled her bike into the crowd and passed three jam jars to Melvin.

He handed one each to Rhubarb and Yoshi. 'Get scooping!' he cried.

'Scooping?' said Rhubarb, stumbling towards the crater. 'Your plan is to scoop that ... **THING** into jam jars?'

'Well yeah,' said Melvin. 'Don't you like it?'

Yoshi patted him on the back. 'It's a great plan, Melv. But don't you think it might eat us if we do that?' he said. 'It doesn't look like the sort of creature that likes being scooped.'

'I spose you've got a point,' said Melvin, peering up at the monster and hearing a familiar whispering sound coming out of it. 'Hey, wait a minute ...'

'What's that noise?' said Yoshi, cupping his ears.

'It's the Donut Hole Monsters,' said Melvin, inching backwards towards the hole. 'They're whispering.'

'What are they saying?' asked Rhubarb.

'I don't know,' said Melvin. 'I heard them doing it to Hector, the other night round at Dirk's.'

Melvin stuffed his hands in his pockets, trying to think. Inside one of them was the Donut Hole Monster packet he and Rhubarb had found.

He thought back to what Violet had said when she'd been standing in his room a few days earlier, looking at all his toy bags.

Melvin nudged Rhubarb. 'I think I know what they're whispering!' he said.

'What is it, Melv?' asked Yoshi. 'Quick, before we all fall into that hole!'

What they were whispering

'Toys are made for playing with,' said Melvin. 'That's why they're whispering to us - they want to be played with!'

'Played with?' said Rhubarb.

The whole crowd listened as the Donut Hole Monsters inside the giant bogey monster whispered their strange song.

'So what if they're whispering something?' cried a big kid three rows back from Melvin. 'I'm a centimetre away from that blooming hole and he's going on about flipping whispers!'

'I think Melvin's right,' said Yoshi. 'They sound sad - the poor things just want to be played with.'

Rhubarb looked behind her at the giant hole. 'What are we gonna do about it?' she said.

Yoshi smiled up at the monster. 'Hey fella,' he said, putting his jam jar down on the floor. 'You wanna play with me?'

The big ball of slime leaned over and ate Yoshi Fujikawa in one bite.

'YOSHI!' screamed Rhubarb, turning to Melvin.
'Melvin Pebble, sometimes you are a complete idiot.'

Melvin picked up Yoshi's jam jar and twisted the
top off, charging forwards.

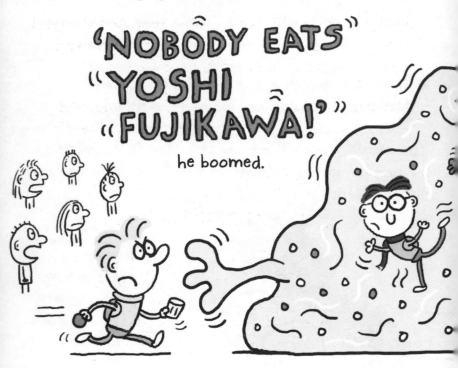

'NOBODY EATS
YOSHI
FUJIKAWA!'

he boomed.

A see-through green arm shot out and knocked
him to the ground.

'It's no good,' shouted Violet. 'You've got to
distract it somehow.'

'But how?' said Rhubarb, stumbling backwards with the crowd of wailing kids.

'I dunno!' cried Violet. 'I thought you were the expert at this stuff?'

Rhubarb stared at the big slime monster. Dwayne, the Cool Doods and now Yoshi were swimming around inside it amongst the glowing toys.

She slung her rucksack off her back, whipped her torch out and started pumping the handle.

'You gonna waggle that thing around to distract it?' asked Melvin.

Rhubarb shook her head. 'Nope,' she said, running up to the monster.

Rhubarb skidded to a stop, a slimy-green-arm's-length away from the giant bogey.

'Fujikawa!' she shouted.

Inside the slime, Yoshi twizzled round.

'Catch this!' called Rhubarb, throwing him the torch. It flew through the air and squodged into the monster with a satisfying

Thwump

Yoshi swam towards the torch and grabbed it. 'Shine it into the toys' eyes!' cried Rhubarb. 'But remember, you've got to squeeze the handle!'

Yoshi started to pump the handle in super-slime-slow-motion and the bulb began to shine. He pointed it into the eyes of the Donut Hole Monster nearest him and the little beast scrunched its eyelids shut.

'Quick Melvin, catch it before it opens its eyes!' called Rhubarb.

Melvin ran over and scooped the toy out of the gunk with the jam jar. 'Got him!' he smiled, twisting the lid back on. The lump of plastic sunk to the bottom of the jar, its eyes turning into crosses.

'Good work!,' said Rhubarb. 'Now we've just got to catch the rest.'

Behind them, the hole rumbled. 'That thing's about to blow!' cried Violet, as a volcano of bolognese exploded into the sky. 'Watch your heads!' she shouted as mud rained down on them all.

Inside the monster, Yoshi was busy shining Rhubarb's torch into the eyes of more Donut Hole Monsters.

Violet threw jam jars out to kids in the crowd.
'What are you waiting for?' she cried.
'Get scooping!'

'HELP ME!' screamed a girl, the backs of her trainers just millimetres away from the hole.

The purple clouds in the sky above crackled, and a bolt of lightning shot out.

'Take this, you naughty little critter!' shouted Rhubarb, scooping a yellow Donut Hole Monster into her jar.

The giant green bogey wobbled like a jelly sitting on a washing machine. 'It's losing its power!' cried Violet, as it roared up at the sky.

The clouds cleared and the moon shone down. 'Look at the size of that thing!' gasped Rhubarb, but Melvin was too busy staring at Yoshi.

No more squeeze

Inside the monster, Yoshi was still holding Rhubarb's torch, but he wasn't pumping the handle any more.

'Can't . . . go . . . on,' he mouthed. 'Hand's . . . too . . . tired . . .'

'Oh no,' cried Rhubarb. 'Yoshi's run out of squeeze!'

Violet pointed at The Cool Doods and Dwayne, who were cowering in a corner of the monster, where its bum would be if it'd had a bum. 'Maybe one of that lot could do it instead?' she said.

Melvin shook his head. 'That won't be quick enough,' he shouted. 'What we need is some kind of giant torch. We've got to dazzle ALL the toys.'

He thought for a second. 'Violet, has that bike of yours got reflectors on it?' he called.

Violet peered down at her bike, then up at the moon. 'Yeah,' she said, smiling. 'Nice idea, little bro!'

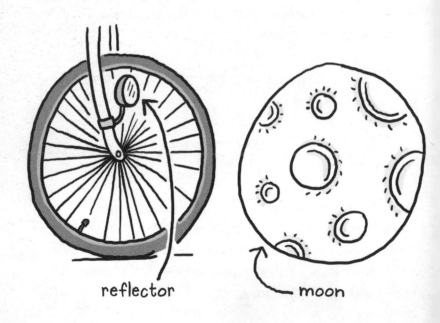

reflector   moon

The bogey monster was still limping towards the hole. 'I'm gonna fall!' cried a kid from the crowd, wobbling on the edge.

Violet gripped the white reflector on the front of her bike and waggled it backwards and forwards a few times until it snapped off.

She held it up in the sky and moved it around until the light from the moon bounced off it, straight into the monster's belly.

The giant ball of snot glowed white and the Donut Hole Monsters inside squeezed their eyes shut.

225

'Good work, Sis!' cried Melvin. 'Now scoop those little critters!'

Hundreds of kids' arms plunged into the monster like mini swords with jam jars on their ends.

Melvin twisted the lid off his jar and squelched it into the monster. He pulled his hand out and Hector's head appeared in the hole left behind.

'Get me out of this thing, Pebbles!' he screamed.

'Sorry Frisbee,' said Melvin, putting the lid back on his jar. 'Bit busy right now.'

There was only one toy left inside the monster now – Rhubarb's golden one. It hovered in the middle of the monster, its eyes scrunched shut.

'This is the last jam jar,' cried Violet, pulling it out of the box.

High up in the sky, the moon was still shining bright. 'Look!' shouted Yoshi. A large crater, dead in the centre of it, was doing something very strange.

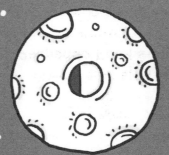

'It's opening up,' cried Rhubarb. 'Just like in my mum's Daily Donut story!'

227

Sure enough, the crater was getting bigger, and now a laser of bright green light was shining out of it, directly into the hole in the middle of Donut Island.

The monster reached a wobbly arm out, sticking it into the beam of light, and he started to glow bright green as well.

The last Donut Hole Monster's eyes snapped open.

'Oh you have got to be kidding me,' said Violet, chucking her reflector at the giant monster's arm. It bounced off and disappeared into the hole.

'Careful, Vi,' shouted Melvin. 'You don't want to annoy it.'

Violet smiled at her brother. 'Oh yes I do,' she said, picking up the empty cardboard box and throwing it in the same direction.

Diving into the monster's bum

The box flew through the air and squodged into the monster's arm.

The giant slime ball roared, shooting out its glowing green hand and picking Violet up.

'NOOO!' cried Melvin, watching as the beastly bogie dangled his sister over the hole.

Rhubarb was looking at the golden Donut Hole Monster. It was zipping around inside the giant ball of snot now, its eyes glowing bright green too.

'We have to catch that toy,' she shouted.

(('HELP ME!'))

cried Violet.

Melvin stared up at his sister. 'This is all my fault,' he said. 'If only I hadn't let Hector grab that golden monster out of my pocket.'

He peered at The Cool Doods, floating around inside the monster's bum.

'What did I ever seen in those losers,' he mumbled to himself, running straight towards it.

"Swimming" down "an" "arm"

It was a strange feeling, diving into a slime monster's bum with a jam jar in your hand.

The screams of a hundred kids switched off and Melvin was floating in a sticky silence. It was actually quite relaxing.

Then a flash of golden plastic zoomed past.

Melvin swam after the Donut Hole Monster, grabbing Rhubarb's torch out of Yoshi's hand as he passed him.

The toy stopped suddenly and twizzled round, hovering just in front of The Cool Doods and Dwayne.

The giant ball of snot carried on wobbling towards the hole, taking them all with it. Melvin peered through the green gunk at the crowd and spotted Rhubarb, teetering on the edge. Violet was still dangling in the sky.

The Donut Hole Monster smiled at Melvin then shot off again, along the arm of the great beast, towards Violet.

I don't even collect the stupid things, thought Melvin, swimming after it. He peered down into the never-ending hole as he floated above it and felt his tummy do a loop-the-loop.

The little golden toy came to a stop at the end of the arm, a centimetre away from Violet.

235

Down below, Rhubarb was shouting something to the crowd of kids. Melvin stared at the evil toy floating in front of him and wondered what to do.

Violet could scoop it up in her jam jar, but that might kill the slime monster.

And seeing as Melvin and his sister were hovering twenty metres above a giant never-ending hole right this millisecond, that didn't seem like a very sensible thing to do.

Then again, if Violet didn't scoop it up, the monster would carry on wobbling towards the hole.

All of a sudden, the enormous arm lurched. Melvin peered at the ground below. A hundred kids' hands were tickling the monster's armpit.

Rhubarb gave him a thumb's up, and Melvin smiled.

The giant bogey's arm jiggled through the air as the crowd carried on tickling. More slimy arms shot out from its body as it tried to swat the kids away.

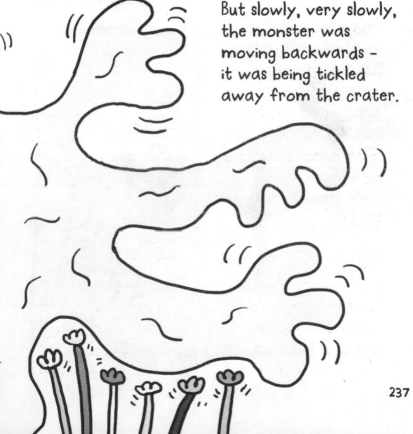

But slowly, very slowly, the monster was moving backwards - it was being tickled away from the crater.

Melvin gripped the torch, waiting for the right moment. He just hoped the little gold toy wouldn't move . . .

The monster shot an arm out lower down and thwacked Rhubarb, tumbling her backwards towards the hole.

She fell over the edge and vanished.

"RHUBARB!"

cried Melvin, but no sound came out of his mouth. Below, the kids waggled their fingers faster and faster. The giant arm flailed as it headed for land.

'NOW!' screamed Violet, not that Melvin could hear her.

He squeezed Rhubarb's torch and pumped the handle. The little gold toy shot back down the monster's arm, trying to escape. But Melvin twizzled in the slime and thrust the torch at the toy, just as the bulb lit up.

The Donut Hole Monster's eyes scrunched shut and Violet thwumped her jam jar into the gunk. 'Got it!' she cried, scooping up the monster and twisting the lid back on her jar.

The Donut Hole Monster sank to the bottom of the jar as the slimy green jelly Melvin was floating in started to break up into little raindrops of goo.

'WAAAHHHH!!!' he screamed, falling through the air and landing with a splodge on the ground next to his big sister.

The big green ray of
light that was shining
into the hole flickered.
Above them, the crater
on the moon began
to close.

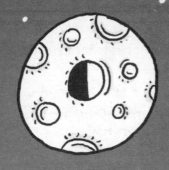

The Cool Doods and
Dwayne were lying in
a giant puddle of bogey
juice a couple of metres
away. All around them
stood the crowd of kids,
covered from head to
toe in gunk.

'W-where am I?' said Hector, scraping slime
out of his ears.

Dirk shook his head, globules of goo spraying
off it. 'I dunno,' he murmured. 'Last thing
I remember, we were in Donut Diner.'

Melvin stared at the crowd of kids. They were peering around as if they were lost.

'It's like they've woken up from a trance or something,' he said.

Yoshi staggered over, pushing his glasses up his nose. 'I need a bath,' he said. 'Or a shower at the very least.'

Melvin hugged his pal. 'Yoshi, can you remember what just happened?'

'What am I, a goldfish?' said Yoshi. 'Course I can remember. Although the sooner I forget about being inside that giant bogey, the better.'

Melvin peered at the jam jars, lying on the floor around him, filled with dead monster toys. 'The trance must've only affected the kids who collected them,' he muttered to himself.

'Hey, where's Rhubarb?' asked Yoshi.

Melvin yelped. 'RHUBARB!' he gasped, remembering her falling into the hole. He sprinted over to the edge of it . . .

... just in time to see the tip of a pair of donut tongs appear. The shiny metal arms pincered a blade of grass. 'Almost ... there ...' warbled a familiar voice, as Rhubarb heaved herself out of the hole.

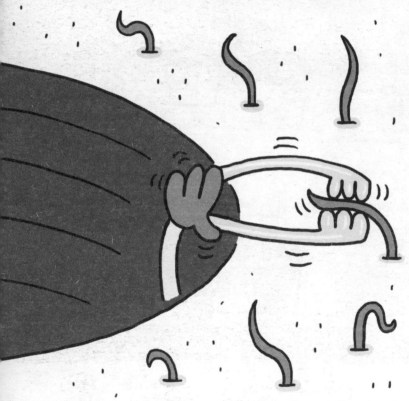

'Rubes!' cried Melvin, giving her a slimy hug. 'Sorry, I forgot you fell in there.'

'Oh that's alright,' said Rhubarb. 'It was only a great big ginormous never-ending hole. Lucky I had these tongs in my back pocket.'

Melvin chuckled. 'We did it, gang,' he said, putting his arm round Yoshi. 'Another mystery solved by the Daily Donut Club!'

Rhubarb smiled. 'We're not quite finished yet, Melv,' she said.

Deirdre's jam jars

'MELVIN!' cried Deirdre Pebble. It was seven o'clock the next morning.

'YEAH?' croaked Melvin from under his duvet.

'GET DOWN HERE RIGHT NOW!' yelled his mum.

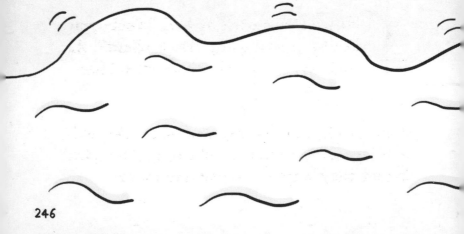

Melvin pulled on his clothes and stumbled down the stairs, wondering if everything that'd happened the night before had been a bad dream.

'Morning, mum,' he smiled, strolling into the kitchen.

His mother stared at him. 'Would you like to explain what THIS is about?' she said, pointing at the shelf behind her.

Melvin looked up. There, lined up on the shelf, was his mum's collection of empty jam jars. Except they weren't empty any more.

Now they were filled with what looked like some kind of green slime. And at the bottom of every one sat a small plastic creature, its eyes scrunched shut.

'Oh right,' said Melvin, looking at his watch. 'Erm, I'm supposed to be somewhere, actually. Can this wait till later, Mum?'

Norman Pebble walked into the room. 'Ooh, that's unusual,' he said, smiling up at the display. 'About time those jam jars had a use.'

Deirdre ignored her husband. 'You do realise I collect

jam jars, don't you, Melvin?' she said.

Violet wandered in, yawning. 'Is this that science project you were telling me about?' she said, looking at the jars.

Melvin smiled at his sister. 'Erm, yeah, that's right,' he said, giving her a nudge.

Norman gave his wife a cuddle. 'I think it's great,' he said. 'Very . . . original.'

Deirdre stepped back and squinted at the shelves. 'Well I suppose I could get used to them,' she said, as Melvin headed for the front door.

Back to "Donut" "Diner"

Melvin skidded to a stop outside Donut Diner. 'Morning, gang!' he smiled, high-fiving Rhubarb and Yoshi.

The purple clouds had floated away and the sun shone in the sky above. Behind the building, there was an enormous great big hole in the ground.

'How about last night,' chuckled Dwayne as Melvin and his pals walked through the door of the restaurant. 'That was pretty crazy, wasn't it!'

Rhubarb nodded. 'That's why we're here,' she said. 'We had a few questions.'

'Oh yeah?' said Dwayne, handing them a donut each.

'Yeah,' said Yoshi, taking a bite. 'Like this one - where did you get the Donut Hole Monsters from?'

Dwayne looked at the three kids standing in front of him and sighed. 'Alright, I admit it,' he said. 'I found them down by the old hole.'

'I knew it!' said Rhubarb, spraying donut crumbs all over the floor.

'I was there the morning after the big storm,' said Dwayne. 'Checking out that giant crack that'd appeared.'

THE MORNING AFTER THE BIG STORM...

Melvin thought back to the night he'd arrived on Donut Island. 'The bolt of lightning,' he said. 'I saw it hit the ground!'

Dwayne nodded. 'The Donut Hole Monsters were just kind of lying there,' he said. 'As if they'd grown out of the earth or something.'

'Except they were in bags, right?' said Yoshi.

FEW SECONDS LATER...

'Right,' said Dwayne. He grabbed a donut for himself and took a great big disgusting chomp on it.

Rhubarb looked at him. 'Why did you take them out of their bags, Dwayne?' she asked. 'What've you got against BAGS?!'

'Nothing,' said Dwayne, chewing. 'They were just muddy, that's all. This is a quality donut establishment I'm running here, I can't serve my customers muddy toys!'

'So that's that, then,' said Melvin, polishing off his donut. 'Mystery solved.'

'Not exactly,' said Yoshi. 'We still don't know where the Donut Hole Monsters came from originally.'

Rhubarb licked a blob of chocolate off her finger. 'I think I might,' she said, and they all leaned in.

Mystery solved

Yoshi whipped his notepad and pen out, waiting for Rhubarb to carry on talking. 'Go on then,' he said. 'Tell us!'

'Well,' said Rhubarb. 'Remember that story in my mum's Daily Donut?'

Melvin thought for a second. 'The one about the van driving into the giant hole?' he said.

'That's it,' said Rhubarb. She grabbed a napkin off the counter and wiped her mouth.

'What about it?' asked Yoshi, eyeing up a second donut.

Rhubarb looked at her two friends.

'It was a "DELIVERY" van,' she said.

'Oh right, yeah,' said Melvin. 'Erm . . . so what?'

'So it was "DELIVERING" something,' smiled Rhubarb.

Yoshi blinked. 'Why do you keep saying it like that, Rubes?' he said.

Rhubarb rolled her eyes. 'What if it was "DELIVERING" Donut Hole Monsters to Donut Diner?' she said.

Dwayne clicked his sugar-covered fingers. 'Hey,' he said. 'That rings a bell, actually.'

'What bell?' said Yoshi, staring at a strawberry coated donut.

'Oh, just a thing my dad told me once,' said Dwayne. 'Something about a delivery going missing when I was a kid. He used to own Donut Diner, you see, and he'd ordered all these little toys to give away with donuts. But they never turned up . . .'

REMEMBER THIS...

Rhubarb looked at Dwayne. 'And you didn't think maybe the Donut Hole Monsters might possibly be those toys?' she asked.

'Nah,' said Dwayne, licking his lips. 'Do you know how busy I am, running this place? I haven't got time to solve mysteries like you lot!'

Melvin imagined the Donut Hole Monsters, bobbling around down at the bottom of the hole for however many years it'd been.

'No wonder they'd gone a bit weird,' he said.

Yoshi stroked his chin. 'Something must've happened to them down there, that's for sure,' he said.

'But what?' said Melvin.

Rhubarb looked at them all. 'You know when the moon shot that beam of light into the giant hole last night?" she asked.

They all nodded.

'It was exactly like in my mum's story,' she said. 'Those werehogs too - there were more of them around during a full moon, remember?'

'So what are you saying, Rubes?' asked Yoshi.

'I think when the moon lines up with the giant hole, it makes super weird stuff happen,' said Rhubarb.

Melvin thought for a second. 'That hole's been filled in for years,' he said. 'No wonder everything's been so boring around here . . . apart from all your mysteries of course!'

'Well, now it's open again,' said Rhubarb.

'I'm just glad we didn't have to deal with any werehogs,' chuckled Yoshi.

Dwayne laughed. 'I don't think I'll be giving away any free toys for a while, that's for sure,' he said.

'Actually,' said Melvin, unzipping his rucksack. 'I wanted to ask you about that.'

He pulled out a shiny little bag. 'I think it's time my toy bag collection found a new home.'

DONUT DINER

Rhubarb gasped. 'WHAT?!' she cried. 'You're giving them away?'

Melvin nodded. 'Toys are made to be played with,' he smiled. 'Besides, I'll be too busy solving mysteries from now on to bother with these.'

'I KNEW you liked mysteries!' said Rhubarb.

Dwayne took the little bag and gave it a fiddle. 'Interesting,' he said, peering out the window at the hole. 'Where'd you get them from, though?'

Melvin chuckled. 'Don't you worry,' he said. 'These ones are safe.'

'Let me give you something for them, at least,' said Dwayne.

Yoshi shot his hand up. 'How about free donuts for life?' he grinned.

Dwayne laughed. 'I'll think about it,' he said.   263

Best title yet!

After that, Melvin, Rhubarb and Yoshi headed to school, Yoshi scribbling away in his notepad the whole way there.

'Finished!' he smiled, as they walked through the gates of Donut Juniors. He ripped a couple of sheets out of the little book and passed them to Rhubarb.

Melvin peered over her shoulder, reading the headline of Yoshi's story. 'Danger At Donut Diner,' he said, reading it out loud. 'Now THAT'S a good title!'

'Best one yet,' said Rhubarb.

Melvin looked at his two best friends. 'Can I say how sorry I am, again?' he said.

Yoshi pushed his glasses up his nose. 'I think you just did, Melvin,' he said. 'Say sorry, that is. When you asked if you could say it.'

Melvin chuckled. 'Really I am,' he said. 'I was an idiot.'

'We forgive you, Pebbles,' said Rhubarb, smiling at him. 'Now can I carry on reading Yoshi's story, please?'

Just then, Melvin spotted The Cool Doods wandering through the school gates.

'Morning, losers,' he called to them. 'How you feeling today?'

'A bit bunged up, to be honest,' said Hector, blowing his nose. 'Think I might have a cold coming on.

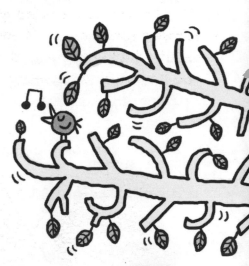

'Oh that's a shame,' said a voice, and Melvin twizzled round. Violet was standing behind the wire fence that separated the junior school from Donut High.

Next to her was a taller girl who looked familiar somehow. 'Vi's been telling me all about what happened,' she said. 'Sounds like you had quite an evening, Hector.'

Hector blinked. 'Eh?' he said. 'What are you talking about?'

The tall girl laughed. 'Don't worry,' she said. 'Your secret's safe with me, little bro.'

Rhubarb finished reading Yoshi's notes and looked up. 'Just brilliant,' she smiled.

Melvin grabbed the sheets of paper. 'Can I borrow them for a second,' he said, running off towards Mr Thursday, who was standing by the gates.

Danger at Donut Diner

It was dark and stormy night

Everybody stood there for a bit until Melvin reappeared with Mr Thursday next to him.

'I just read this,' said their teacher, holding up Yoshi's story. 'It's fantastic, guys. What imagination!'

'Imagination?' said Rhubarb, smiling at Melvin and Yoshi. 'Oh, yes, IMAGINATION!'

Mr Thursday grinned. 'Have you ever thought about doing a proper school newspaper?' he asked. 'Melvin here seems to think we've got some old printers hidden away somewhere.'

Rhubarb gasped. 'What do you reckon, gang?' she asked.

'I'm up for it!' grinned Yoshi, and Melvin nodded.

'Course, we'll have to find some new mysteries,' he said, sniffing the air.

Rhubarb nudged him. 'Oh, I don't think that'll be a problem,' she said, leaning in so only Melvin and Yoshi could hear.

'After all,' she whispered, 'everybody knows Donut's not an ordinary town . . .'

Watch out for the return of The Daily Donut Club in...

"Attack of the haunted lunchbox"

A SUPER WEIRD! ™

MYSTERY

Read my other books - or don't!

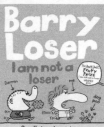

Spellchecked by
Jim Smith

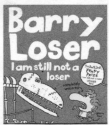

Commas put in by
Jim Smith

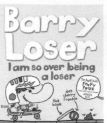

Noses drawn by
Jim Smith

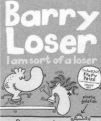

Pages numbered by
Jim Smith

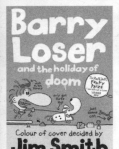

Colour of cover decided by
Jim Smith

Produced and directed by
Jim Smith

Absolutely nothing to do with
Jim Smith

From the squidgy pink brain of
Jim Smith

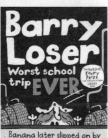

Banana later slipped on by
Jim Smith

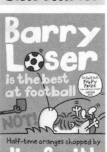

Half-time oranges chopped by
Jim Smith

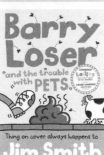

Thing on cover always happens to
Jim Smith

Written by robots controlled by
Jim Smith

Really badly wrapped up by
Jim Smith

Jim Smith

Jim Smith

Jim Smith